"CRY FIRE"

Short Stories of a New York City Firefighter

By

Andrew Ashurst

ISBN: 1-4107-1710-0 (e-book)
ISBN: 1-4107-1929-4 (Paperback)
ISBN: 1-4107-3916-3 (Dust Jacket)

This book is printed on acid free paper.

1st Books - rev. 04/14/03

Dedication

This book is dedicated to firefighters everywhere , be it

professional or volunteer, and to those men with Engine

216, 108 Truck , 35th Battalion

and the 11th. Division that I had the honor to work with and

to all my

brothers of the New City Fire Department who lost their

lives in the

performance of their duties especially to the Brothers who

lost their

lives at the World Trades Center September 11, 2001.

This book is also dedicated to all the families of firefighters

and emergency

response teams everywhere, and especially to those who

lost their loved ones in the performance of their duties.

A portion of the proceeds from the sale of this book will be

contributed to

The New York City Firefighters Burn Unit

These stories are true accounts

Some of the names of the fire fighters and response areas

have been changed .

Acknowledgements

I would like to thank my wife Chris and my children for their support and encouragement they gave me in writing this book.

I would also like to thank my close friend, Battalion Chief Frank Ryan F.D.N.Y for his support, my late friend Rich Caggiano who was a retired disabled New York City firefighter. His support and encouragement for me will always be remembered.

125 YEARS OF SERVICE TO WILLIAMSBURG
ENGINE 216

Williamsburg was first settled in 1660 when Dutch framers laid out farms. The City of Brooklyn annexed the Village of Williamsburg in 1855. This new area would become known has the "Eastern District".

Five years after the end Civil War. Brooklyn replaced its volunteer fire department with a fully paid department. Thirteen engine companies and six ladder companies would replace the sixty-three volunteer fire companies. The Eastern District would include Engines 11(now 211), 12(212), 13(213) and Ladders 4(104), 5(105), and 6(106).

In 1872 America looked and acted a little different than today. The United States had only 37 states in the Union. Ulysses S. Grant would be elected to his second term as the President of the United States. The Transcontinental Railroad linking the East Coast with the West Coast was three years old and Indian Wars on the Great Plains was just beginning. Famous names familiar to us today were unknown in 1872; Alexander Graham Bell, General George Custer, Teddy Roosevelt, Thomas Edison and the Wright Brothers.

The Brooklyn Fire Department would remain the same that year. Engine 2(202) and Ladder 1(101) were combined into a new house, the first for the BFD. They also would add three new engine companies to the growing City. Engine 14(214) was placed in service on July 4 in a new house.

On Sept 15, 1872, the BFD placed two new fire companies in service in the Greenpoint and Williamsburg sections. The population of these two areas was spreading out further from the center of town as new people moved into the area. With this migration the fire department needed more companies. Engine 15(215) was located in Greenpoint and Engine 16(216) in the southern section of Williamsburg.

The fire protection in Williamsburg was provided by Ladder 5(105), located at Manhattan Avenue and Ten Eyck Street, Engine 13(213) at Powers Street and Graham. Ladder 4(104) was in the center of Williamsburg on S. 3rd Street. Engine 16 was placed in the former volunteer quarters of Eagle Engine Company No. 6, located on Stagg Street near Union. The house was built around 1854 for Bucket Company 6 and Engine 6 moved into the house replacing the Bucket Company a short time later. Around the corner on Scholes Street was Continental Hose 6.

The members of Engine 216 in 1892

During 1873 Ladder 5(105) was disbanded, leaving the area with only Ladder 4(104) to the north. Five years after Engine 16 was organized the Fire Department placed Engine 18(218) in service at 112 Seigel Street on November 30, 1877. The need for a ladder company in this section of Williamsburg was great and ladder 8(108) replaced Engine 18 on Seigel Street. Engine 18 was moved to new quarters at 650 Hart Street on December 1, 1887.

The old house of Engine 16 was in such dilapidated condition that plans for a new house were drawn up. The former house of Continental Hose 6 on Scholes was torn down and a new fire station was built. The lot was purchased from Mark Fowler and his wife for $800 on July 18, 1856. In 1893 Engine 16 moved into the new building at 16 Scholes Street. The two-story house cost $10,000 to build on the 25 x 100-foot lot.

Scholes Street

After the new look

The fire station was the standard style Brooklyn house. The first floor had room for the apparatus and stalls for the horses. In the rear was the feed room and horse supplies. The house watch was located up front and on one side wall were the racks for drying out the hoses. Upstairs had three rooms, one room for the officer, a bunkroom with built in lockers for the firemen and a recreation room.

One hundred and twenty-five years ago the fireman life was a hard one. He would work 24 hours a day for seven days and have the eight day off. He could go home for meals twice a day. During his hours at the firehouse the time was taken up with housewatch duty, hydrant inspection, messenger service, detail to other companies for meals, house cleaning chores, and taking care of the horses. The salary for a first grade fireman was $700 a year or $13.46 a week for the 168 hour work week.

The Cities of New York (including the Bronx), Brooklyn, Long Island City, parts of Western Queens, and Staten Island merged into the five Boroughs of New York City on January 1, 1898. Engine 16 officially became part of the FDNY on January 26th. On October 1, 1899, Engine 16 was renumbered to Engine 116 to avoid confusion with Engine 16 in Manhattan. The ladder companies were given fifty to their number and Ladder 1 became Ladder 51. Engine 116

was renumbered to Engine 216 on January 1, 1913.

After WW II the Fire Department started a rebuilding program. The front wall of Engine 216 cracking and needed replacing. It's not known when it was rebuilt but it gave the house a new look. By the late fifties the station was in need of being replaced. A study on fire station locations also recommended that many stations could be closed and the companies combined. One of these studies recommended that Engine 237 and Ladder 108 be relocated into a new house on Seigel Street near White Street and Bushwick Avenue. A new combined fire and police station was built at 187 Union Avenue off of Broadway. Ladder 108 moved in on August 9, 1971 along with Battalion 35. Engine 216 relocated from Scholes Street on October 13, 1971

Engine 216 has had four members of the company receiving medals for acts of bravery. Fireman Frederick Schultz received the Brooklyn Citizens Medal for rescuing a woman and her two children from a fire at 190 Meserole Street on January 17, 1905. The Walter Scott Medal was awarded to Fireman John C. Baal on July 1, 1967. He rescued a man from a window via a scaling ladder at 53 Scholes Street. While off duty Fireman Andrew J. Ashurst received the LaGuardia Medal for his rescue of four people from 393 S. 3rd Street on January 20, 1969. Lieutenant Williams H. Hayes rescued six occupants of

x

164 Havemeyer Street on July 11, 1992 and was awarded the Trevor - Warren Medal. He was doing a mutual in Ladder 108 when he made his rescue. Beside these four medals the Company have earned a total of fifteen Unit Citations.

Tragedy struck the company twice with members losing their lives during the performance of their duty. On January 14, 1880, Captain William Baldwin was injured while fighting a fire in Otto Huber Brewery, a three story wood frame building, at 263 Montrose Avenue. The fire was out in less than thirty minutes, and was being placed under control, when without warning, the rear of the building collapsed. Six firemen were injured in the collapse with two being serious. Captain Baldwin was trapped under a beam and received internal injuries along with cuts and bruises. He was removed to St. Catherine's Hospital where he died on January 20 and was buried in Evergreen Cemetery. Captain Baldwin lived at 422 South

4th Street and left a wife and three children. He joined the Department in 1872 and had been the Captain of Engine 16 since 1875. Baldwin was the first member of the Brooklyn Fire Department to lose his life in the line of duty.

The second member to lose his life was Lieutenant Raymond Schiebel of Engine 221. He was working overtime in Engine 216 on the night of March 5, 1995. The company was operating at 128 Hayward Street in a heavy smoke condition when Lt. Schiebel suffered a heart attack. He died on March 7 from the effects of the heart attack. He lived in Bethpage, Long Island with his wife and three children.

Engine 216 has served the Community of Williamsburg faithfully for the past 125 years. No matter what the need was, a fire, or emergency the Company was always ready to protect the citizens of New York City.

THE WHEELS OF ENGINE 216

18?? Amoskeag 2nd size steamer
1869 Amoskeag 2 wheel hose wagon, rebuilt in 1884
1882 Amoskeag 2nd size steamer
1894 Amoskeag 2nd size steamer
1895 Marlborough hose wagon
1901 LaFrance 3rd size steamer
1901 P. J. Barrett hose wagon
1921 American LaFrance 700 gpm pumper, Oct. 20, 1921
1927 International/Pirsch hose wagon, Nov. 7, 1927
1938 Ward LaFrance hose wagon, June 17, 1938
1939 Ward LaFrance 1000 gpm pumper, Jan. 28, 1939
1947 Mack 750 gpm used as hose wagon, Feb.16, 1954
1946 Ward LaFrance 750 gpm used as hose wagon, July 2, 1959
1960 Ward LaFrance 1000 gpm pumper, Sep. 9, 1960

1968 Mack 1000 gpm pumper, Mar. 20, 1969
1972 Mack 1000 gpm pumper, Dec. 4, 1972
1975 Mack 1000 gpm pumper, Oct. 9, 1975
1980 American LaFrance 1000 gpm pumper, Apr. 14, 1981
1986 Mack/Ward 79 1000 gpm pumper, Jan. 14, 1987

1986 Mack/Ward 79 1000 gpm pumper

March 10, 1973 at 12:55 A. M . The voice alarm blared out " Engine 216, 108

Truck turn out to Box 337 a working fire at 173 Hayward Street.

The reaction was automatic as the members of Engine 216 and 108 Truck respond.

In twenty seconds both Engine 216 and 108 Truck are out of quarters and Heading down towards Hayward Street. Little did I know that this would be the fire which would end my career as a New York City Firefighter.

We arrived at Hayward Street and saw fire blowing out from the windows on the top floor of a three-story brownstone building. Engine 216 pulled into the street first, so we could hook up to a fire hydrant close to the building on fire. 108 Truck came in after us to position the ladder in front of the building. When we got to the hydrant the chauffer jumped out of the cab of the Engine and with one of the members took off the soft suction hose and attached it to the hydrant. As we were donning our masks and tanks, I noticed a group of men by us. One of them yelled over to us and said , " Have fun when you go in fireman"

I didn't like the feeling that I got from those men and told the Lieutenant that we should be careful, I don't like the vibes that those guys over there gave us.

We stretched the line off the truck and up the outside stairs, and into the building . Engine Co 211 arrived second due at the scene.

The fire up on the third floor involved the rear rooms of the floor but was pushing towards the front of the building. We started to ascend the stairway, pushing the fire back as we approached the third floor. I was the second man on the line and we were almost to the top of the stairs when everything broke loose, the whole stairway collapsed under us. All I could remember was free falling backwards and my arms and legs hitting things. The next thing that I was aware of, was that I was lying on my back in the basement . I must have blacked out, because I didn't remember hitting bottom. Then I remember laying on my back in the basement of the building, looking up and seeing an inferno above me. I heard somebody moaning near me. I turned to my side and saw from the reflection of the fire that it was one of the guys from my company, his leg seemed to be caught in some sub flooring .

I got on my knees, lifted him up and said, " Jerry it's me , Andy , let me help you up. When Jerry was able to move, he took off , out of the building. When I tried to get up and leave the area myself I felt a shock of pain in my back and saw stars. As if somebody lit up a Fourth of July sparkler. I must have passed out for a second or two.

When I came around, I was afraid to move figuring the fall must have done damage to my back , and aggravated it when I helped out Jerry .

It seemed like an eternity before someone came looking for me. Then I heard somebody yelling out to me. It was one of the members of 108 Truck, Pudgy Walsh. I yelled back so that he could find me. He found me on the floor, I yelled that my back is injured and in pain. Pudgy told me to hang in there and that he would be back in short time. Pudgy came back with some of the members of 108, and they put me in a stokes basket so that I wouldn't move and got me outside. Rescue 2 was on the scene and was ready to take the injured members to the hospital.

The members of Rescue Co. 2 and 108 Truck helped the injured members of Engine 216 into Rescue 2 truck so that they could get us to the hospital.

The ride to the hospital with my injured brothers was the third ride to a hospital for me as a firefighter. I pondered what the outcome of this injury might mean to my career .The other members were treated and released from the hospital and were taken back to 216's quarters . I was kept in the hospital with a possible spinal injury. As I laid in my bed I started thinking back to when I first started the job.

IT ALL BEGINS

The war in Vietnam is going strong, many of our soldiers are coming home in body bags. The protesters are rampaging our cities, parts of Detroit, New York, and Watts L.A are in flames, insurrection and riots abound, and the worst is yet to come.

It's the summer of 1967 and I am a Sanitation worker for the City of New York and I am working the evening shift. I'm on the job about two and half years . With virtually no seniority on the job, I am always detailed to other Sanitation Districts to collect garbage. I am sure that I have picked up every garbage can in Brooklyn New York.

I needed a steady job so I applied and took tests for the Police Dept, Fire Dept and Sanitation Dept. The Sanitation Dept. was the first to call me, but my eyes were on the New York City Fire Dept.

I was never a fire buff or hung out around firehouses, but when I was young lad I was always impressed with the firefighters, watching them battle fires when they occurred in my old neighborhood.

Today, I am detailed with two of my co-workers to take a truck over to Bedford Stuvyesant and collect garbage. Ray Marino and Rudy Smith are my partners today, and we would take turns in driving the truck, this would give us a break every couple of blocks. It was a Monday and as usual the garbage was heavy, (a lot of it). Something was wrong today, I could feel it in the air. When we were collecting garbage in the Brownsville section of Brooklyn I could see black men gathering on the street corners, more than usual. There was a lot of unrest about them , and it started to get us concerned . Rudy said, " I have a bad feeling about this, we had better be alert". This coming from Rudy a black man made Ray and I a little nervous.

The only thing we had to protect us, was a pipe we had jammed in under some steel bands on the side of the truck. The next building we pulled up to was at the corner, it was a four story tenement building and five men were milling around at the corner . There were four cans outside, two with regular garbage and two with cinder ashes. Ray and I each took a can of cinders apiece, because they were heavy, and Rudy took the two cans of lighter garbage. At this point a group of men approached Ray and I from the corner and said," Hey man, how comes the blackman is carrying two cans and you white boy's are carrying one can ? Rudy got that worried look on his face and didn't say a word , and in two seconds Ray and I dropped the cans of cinder and jumped into the truck. Rudy jumped on the back step and yelled take off. We took off with Rudy hanging on the back step of the truck.

We got as far as five blocks away and spotted our Foreman in his vehicle waving us down. He sticks his head out of his window and yells to us, I want all the trucks and men off the streets and back to their districts, riots are breaking out all around town and it could be dangerous for you guys working in this area. At this time Rudy jumps off of the back and joins Ray and I up front . Rudy say's I'm sorry I didn't say anything to those guys back there, but if I opened my mouth they would considered me an Uncle Tom and jumped me. This was the beginning of what we called the War Years in the City.

PROBY SCHOOL

The next day I was off work. It was a beautiful day in Brooklyn New York. I can feel the brisk cool breeze blowing in from the Northwest as I sat on the stoop of my house, waiting for the mailman to show. My mind drifts back to and old T.V. show that I used to watch. It was a story of an old philanthropist who used to give away million dollar checks. But, what I was waiting for, wasn't a million dollar check, but a letter from the New York City Fire Dept. saying that I was accepted as a Probationary Firefighter.

After almost three years the new eligibility list was finally established, and I wasn't too far from the top of the list. This was my one and only chance to make the fire department, because I would be too old for the next test. Sal the postman finally arrives and say's to me , " I think I have what you've been waiting for. I said to Sal, " Are you serious, is it a letter from the New York City Fire Department "?

Sal says " Here take a look". Sure enough it was a letter from the F.D.

I ripped the envelope open , and it read that I was accepted as a Probationary Firefighter and had to report downtown for a physical .

At that time the F.D.N.Y. Firefighting School was located on an island on the East River, situated in between the Boroughs of Queens and Manhattan. This island was called, Welfare Island.

To get to Welfare Island I had to travel through an area called Williamsburg and Bushwick. As I traveled through this area I noticed all the burned out buildings, and windows charred black from fire. The fire companies were always on the move in this area. As I approached the East River I spotted Welfare Island .There is a little bridge that extends out to Welfare Island and is dwarfed by a much larger bridge called the 59th St. Bridge that stretches from Manhattan to 59 St. in Queens.

There is a stark difference between Manhattan and Queens. Manhattan with its towering skyscrapers with walls of masonry and glass, the 59th street bridge loomed over Welfare Island as it stretched from the Borough of Queens to Manhattan Island like a helpless sand dune lying in the East River, and the Queens side, with apartment houses and loft buildings mingled in, here and there.

Just on the other side of the bridge to the Island lays the Fire Dept. Training Center.

I pulled into the training center parking lot and parked my car. At this time the new recruits were pouring into the parking lot. For the next eight weeks these men would be my new brothers in training. I haven't had this feeling since Boot Camp when I joined the Navy . But this time we would be training to fight the enemy, "Fire." Later on I would learn that fire was not the only enemy that a New York City Firefighter had to contend with. As I walked towards the Administration Building I noticed a large group of probies doing their morning calisthenics out on the grinder. These men would be graduating soon, and sent out to their new assignments with various companies.

Instead of G.I. greens the men had on dungarees , fire helmets and fireboots. The Lt. instructing them sounded like a Marine D.I. and had a patch covering one of his eyes, giving him the appearance of a Buccaneer, especially with the boots and helmet on. I found out later that he lost the sight of his eye from a piece of broken glass at a fire. I believe it was because of his misfortune that eyeshields were placed on the helmets of New York City firefighters.

When I entered the Administration building. A firefighter directed me to a large lunchroom where I found all the new recruits. A Firefighter checking us in told us that the coffee and donuts were on the house and that we all would be sworn in soon.

It was a proud feeling I had looking at the men that I would spend the next eight weeks training with because I knew it took a special kind of a man to be a firefighter. About twenty minutes later we were called into a large room to take the oath.

It was now official, I was now a New York City Fireman, but not a firefighter yet.

That would come later after the real on the job experience at my assigned company. Training started the next day at 0900, the day was set aside mostly for measurements of our uniforms and turnout clothing. We were also instructed on what our routine will be for the next ten weeks.

The next day, serious training began, tardiness would not be tolerated and we had to be on the grinder for role call and calisthenics at 0700 hrs. I would get to know the grinder (blacktop) well , because it would take 10-15 lbs off my hide.

We finished calisthenics off by running a mile with our fire-boots on. This was done to buildup our legs to carry the weight of our boots with ease.

After running we were divided up into squads , these would be the men that I would become closest with during training.

The next day we got to meet the Chief in charge of operations known as the Bear. The Bear looked like a cross between a bulldog and a bear. He was as serious about training as he looked. He knew that soon these men under his charge will be under fire, to say the least. I would grow to admire and respect this man and will always remember him as my first boss on the Fire Dept.

When The Bear spoke all eyes were on him , he knew the second you were not attentive. One day I was up on a platform practicing the one man slide, similar to what a mountain climber would use to repel down a cliff. As I climbed up onto the parapet to get ready to descend, I didn't notice the Bear at the bottom checking me out. When I came off the parapet I damned near got my right hand and glove caught under the roof rope. This was a no ,no, because my hand would have been pinned under the rope with all my weight on it, leaving me dangling in the air.

The Bear said in a loud gruffly voice to me, " Try that on the tower, and I'll leave you up there." I almost melted with the look he gave me.

The weeks passed by and we were almost into December. The Proby class was shaping up real good, we were beginning to look like firefighters. The weather was getting bitter cold and damp as the wind blew off the East River.

My squad spent the last three days learning all about the mask, a self-contained breathing apparatus, used in heavy smoke conditions.

When I first arrived on the job, all first due engine companies responding, went into the buildings without masks on, especially if there were civilians trapped in the building . This was to get water on the fire as soon as possible. Later on this procedure was stopped because of the plastics involved in fires.

Today was the evolution at the Smoke House. We would get an idea how it was in a building fully charged with smoke.

Inside the building a 150 lb. Dummy was placed to be rescued. Once the dummy was rescued we had to perform a mock CPR on the dummy.

The first trip into the Smoke House was with masks on. The second trip into the Smoke House was without masks on. We had a charged hose line snaked out through the rooms and eventually led us out side were we would open up the nozzle to get the feel of the nozzle pressure. All the procedures were done in a controlled setting to keep injuries down. Fighting fires was not for a person who suffered from claustaphobia .

There have been instances where firefighters have died in fires because they panicked and pulled off their masks.

A buddy system, if possible, was important, and it was the officers duty to know where his men were at all times.

When we entered the Smoke House without the mask, the smoke came rolling out, the officer in charge ordered us in, this is when they separate the men from the boys.

The trick was to breath slowly through your nose and not to panic, your eyes start burning from the smoke, and tears give you a protective coating for your eyes as you struggle through the rooms keeping your hands on the hose stretched in serpentine fashion throughout the rooms. There is no way that you can hold your breath and make it through the rooms. Holding your breath would only make things get worse. Eventually we make it to the end, and out the door we scramble coughing and choking with soot running down our noses. The fresh air is life, and to panic is to die. But in this situation we had a training officer in the building watching over us like a mother hen. At a real fire we have our brother firefighters looking out for each other, and also our Guardian Angels.

I thought about those poor victims trapped in buildings and unable to find their way out, praying that a firefighter like an angel from heaven would find and rescue them.

The next day our squad was up on the roof of the training tower. Marty was our instructor, he was a first grade firefighter and was our instructor on roof rope techniques.

Marty was a robust Irish man with a great sense of humor who put you at ease when it was your time to go over the ledge. Marty was by the ledge called a parapet, he was waiting with a bright smile and rosy cheeks. Okay guys step right up, don't be bashful you have a net five stories down to catch you .

After my first descent it was a snap, I couldn't get up fast enough to try it again.

Our next evolution with the roof rope, was lowering each other down to the net, this was tricky. You had to have complete confidence in your brother firefighter.

One of the guys in my squad Jim Fury said to me " Hey Andy, I guess I'm going to lower you, ha. Yeah , I said , "I'm under your tender loving care " just don't decide to scratch yourself when I'm over the parapet. The trip down was almost as exciting as the parachute jump at Coney Island.

The next day we got the word that a T.V. celebrity was coming to the training center. We found out that it was Johnny Carson.

Johnny Carson arrived at the center in a couple of days. He wanted to experience first hand what a firefighter goes through when he's in training.

I got to hand it to the man . He got involved with some of the evolutions that we trained for in short time. One day we sent him into the smoke house, fully outfitted in turnout clothes and without a mask on, as he wished. In thirty seconds he came blasting out of the doorway choking and gasping for air. After he recovered from that experience, we gave him a nozzle with charged line. A couple guys backed him up on the nozzle.

We opened up the door of the smoke house fully charged with smoke, Okay Johnny, one of instructors yells out . " Open up the nozzle and attack the fire in the building". Carson, opens up the nozzle and almost loses control of the nozzle hanging on for dear life. It was a sight to see. We were all gathered around him, and couldn't stop from laughing. One evolution Johnny tried was climbing the scaling ladders. We had a training building that rose six stories up. One of the training officers asked me and a couple of other men to go up with him.

I was standing next to Carson and asked him if he'll be okay. He said , "No problem I've been practicing all week. I was the second man up, and Carson was next to go up, he had to grab a scaling ladder and lift it up to me so that I could pass it up to the man above me so that he could place it in the window opening. After we placed the ladder. We all move up the to next floor and snapped the clip of our safety belt on to the neck of the scaling ladder . Johnny Carson was right on my heels, raising the next ladder to be placed above us. We all made it to the top without any problems. Johnny Carson did good. Carson also did the one man slide down from the roof to the ground with no problems . We all had a lot of respect for the man. He had a lot of guts. The last week of our training arrived and all the brothers were notified that a list of our assigned Fire Companies was available, and was pinned up in the cafeteria.

I was assigned to Engine 216. It was an engine company located on Scholes St. in Williamsburg Brooklyn. Engine 216 was in the 35th. Battalion and 11th Div.

Williamsburg was one of the areas that I drove through to get to Proby school.

It was a cold January day when I arrived at Engine 216 quarters. I parked my car in the street close to quarters , this was a bad area with a high rate of stolen cars . I looked down the street and it was lined with three and four story wood frame dwellings and covered on the outside with shingles, I thought to myself (real fire traps).

This was a poor neighborhood with mostly Hispanic people living in it. I noticed a building with the top floor gutted a few houses down. I said to myself these guys fight fires from their front door.

I opened up the door of my car and pulled out my brand new uniforms and turn out clothes, shut the door and walked up to the wooden door and knocked.

A fireman opened the door looking at me with my hands full of gear, and helped me in. I introduced my self as a new member and he yelled back to the kitchen where the other brothers were gathered and said " The new Proby is here."

He introduced himself as Fireman Joe Cass , and said "Come on back and meet the other guys, the Captain is up in his office, but first have a cup of coffee with us in the kitchen, and I'll introduce you to the men. As I walked towards the kitchen I could smell the smoke in the firehouse from the turnout coats hanging on the wall along the way. The turnout coats were blistered from the heat and so were the leather helmets that lay on the rack above each turn out coat. Some of the turnout coats had leather patch pockets replacing the original pockets I said to myself (I think I'm going to break my cherry real fast with this company.)

The first man I met was a stocky guy by the name of Frank O'Malley, Frank reminded me of this actor Pat O'Brien, he looked a bit like him and had a quiet way like him. The next guy that I was introduced to was doing bench presses with about 200 lbs. on the bar. He put the weights in place and came over to greet me, his name was Charlie Benni. Charlie was about 5'9'' and well built, it was important to stay in good shape because it was a tough job, that demanded a lot of physical strength. Charlie welcomed me aboard. Another brother was drinking coffee and got up from the table and introduced himself to me as Tony Amito. Tony said, "give the man a cup of coffee" There's one more guy that you have to meet besides the Captain and he's taking a break in the bunk room. With that I sat down and had a cup of good hot coffee. Before I could say a word, an alarm came in and Engine 216 had to respond, I wasn't assigned a group yet and had to stay put. The Captain yelled out to me while he was putting on his gear, stick around Andy , we'll be back shortly.

I yelled out that I would close the doors. The Mack engine pulled out with sirens screaming heading down Scholes St. I closed the doors to the apparatus floor and sat down in the kitchen to finish my coffee.

The Engine was back in fifteen minutes. The men jumped off the rig to hold up any traffic so that the Engine could back into quarters. The Captain climbed out of the rig and came back to the kitchen to greet me. "Hi Andy, I'm Captain George Scheer, when you get a chance come up to the office and I'll you give a group number, a bunk and a locker for your gear. Your turnout gear can be placed on the rack by the stairs on the apparatus floor. I finished my coffee and excused myself with the other men and climbed

27

the stairs up to the Captains office. Come on in and make yourself comfortable said the Captain. I understand that you were a Sanman prior to the coming on the Fire Dept. Yes I said, Although picking up garbage cans is a steady job, it's not what I really want for a career. The Capt. responded and said, " There will be many times that you wished that you were picking up garbage cans again, Andy. You're probably right, I said, but I'll take it one day at a time. I looked around the office and out to the bunk room and noticed how old the interior was and said to the Capt. "This fire house really goes back in time doesn't it'? Yes it does Andy, it goes back to the days when we had horse drawn pumpers. Andy, the Captain continued. You'll be working with darned good firefighters, listen to their suggestions and you'll learn the ropes, which will help you on the job. As a Proby at fires I want you to stay close to the officer who is working the tour for the day.

28

The Captain said that I will be joining the rest of the new

Probes for two weeks of inspection duties . Some of the

divisions have fallen back in building inspections, because

of the rapid increase in fire duty. You guys are what the

doctor ordered. So I'll see you back in a couple of weeks,

you'll be signed to group 17. Here's a copy of a group chart

so that you know when your is due into work. Lots of luck

Andy, and welcome aboard. .

I went down the old wooden stairs to the Apparatus floor

and went back into the kitchen to have another cup of

coffee with the brothers.

John Cass said come on Andy I'll show you around. We

walked out to the Appartus Floor and John gave me a short

tour of the Engine and were all the tools were located in the

Engine compartments. Go in to the kitchen and grab your

turnout gear and I'll show you where they go. After I came

out of the kitchen with the gear John escorted me to the rack and shelves along side the wall that I saw when I entered the firehouse. " Here's a spot for you , you can hang your coat up here and put your helmet above your coat. You can lay your boots on the floor below your coat.

I said to John, " What a difference in the looks of my turnout gear compared to the others that look real salty" John said back to me, " Believe me Andy, it won't take long before your gear looks the same.

THE INFERNO I MISSED

One day while on my two week inspection tour, I thought to myself. Tonight would be my first night tour with Eng.216. I wonder how it would have gone.

Would I have had my first fire tonight. What kind of a night would I have? Would it be a quite uneventful night?

As a pondered this, a cold chill came over me as a cold wind blew up the street where I was doing my building inspections. The temperature was dropping rapidly, a severe cold front was moving in from the northwest. The district that I was working was in the 10th. Division. This area was considered the Red Hook area of Brooklyn. It was a middle class area with a mixture of ethnic backgrounds. The area was also had a busy shopping and business area.

The day was done and I was glad to get home and get off the cold streets. January is always a cold month in the city. I remember not too long ago, not too far from this area two airliners collided in the air and one plane fell to the streets.

I'll never forget the structure that it hit, " The Pillar of Fire Church. " Till today I think about that tragedy. (But that tragedy would be eclipsed in the future with 9/11). When I got home and sat down to dinner I told the wife , " you know hon , tonight would have been my first night tour with engine 216. The wife replied, " You should be glad your not working tonight it's below freezing out there . Yes, but I was thinking," Would I have been baptized with my first fire tonight?"

The next day I got the news that there was a terrible fire down in Williamsburg, and that nine people were killed including children . There were also reports of firemen injured and rescues made.

That evening after my tour of inspection duty I drove over to Eng. 216 to check on the brothers. Some of the men working tonight were not working last night because of the shift in groups. I only recognized Fr. Joe Cass, Fr. Charlie Benni and Fr. Tony Amito the rest of the men were new to me. Joe Cass recognized me when I entered the apparatus floor, the man on house watch duty was new to me, so Joe introduced him to me, Andy this is fireman Ron Hinks, there's a couple of guys in the kitchen that you haven't met yet so let's go back.

When I got back to the kitchen there was an officer and another fireman who looked like he may be one of the senior members of the company. Joe ushered me over to the officer and introduced me to him. Lt. Munda this is Andy, our new Proby. " Hey, glad to meet you Andy," this fellow is Phil Appeles one of our engine chauffeurs and one of our gourmet' cooks. Phil said to me, would you like to be in on the meal? Sure I answered, this will be my first meal in the firehouse.

Phil said, how come you came in today, Andy? I heard about the bad fire last night and wanted to check on the brothers.

Lt. Munda said, everyone is ok , thank God, just some smoke inhalation, one of the members made a rescue last night. I understand it would have been your first night tour with 216, you would have broke your cherry bigtime last night. Lt. Mundi continued, The Capt. happens to be upstairs doing some paper work. I think he wants to talk to you since you're in quarters. Sure thing Lou, I'll head upstairs now.

As I started up the stairs Lt. Munda yells up to me "Stop in the kitchen for a cup of coffee after you talk with the Captain" Sounds good I yelled back down to the Lt.

When I got to the office I gave a knock on the door the Captain said come on in.

When I entered the office, the Captain was surprised to see me . " Andy, how come you're here today? Answering I said, Thought I'd drop by . I heard about the fire last night. And was wondering how everybody was? The Captain responded

"It's a good thing in a way, that you weren't at that fire. I don't believe you would have been ready for this one as your first fire. It was too much fire for a new guy right out of proby school. I'd like to see you break in a little easier than that.

After the meal, I had some coffee with the brothers and left to get back home.

But before going back home, I decided to go to the scene of the fire. When I got to the scene it looked like a glacier covering a charred remnant of a six story tenement bldg. The fire started in the early morning in a paper box factory located on the bottom floor, above were all occupied

35

apartments. The firefighters were hampered by the wind ,

and sub-zero weather . I can still see hose frozen fast under

the ice. This was a job for the Fire Dept.Thawing Unit.

They'll come and apply steam to the hose to melt the ice, so

that the engine companies can remove their hoses. The fire

started in the early morning hours , when most people were

sleeping. Many civilians were trapped above the fire.

Thanks to the efforts of the responding fire companies

many lives were saved . Engine 216 was first due at the fire.

I can't imagine the feeling inside the men when they saw

this fire, knowing that scores of families, men, women and

children were trapped above the fire.

One of the members of Engine 216 made a rescue using

a scaling ladder. His name was John Ball. John Ball would

be the man that I would replace, he was on the Lieutenants

list and was promoted to Lieutenant while I was on the

inspection team. Soon my two weeks with the inspection

would be over, and I would be back active with my company . I couldn't wait.

Finally, my first tour with Eng. 216. It was a day tour, cold but sunny. It wasn't to busy at this time, just a couple of false alarms. I spent time getting familiar with the firehouse, the Engine, and doing my duties expected of a Proby, and of course having coffee with the brothers. I was shooting the breeze with Tony , and thinking to myself "Will I get my first fire today"?

Tony must have read my thoughts. " Andy ,do you think today is the day? Good chance I replied, good chance. An alarm comes in, it's a special building box, usually this means a factory, School, etc. Ron, who is at housewatch yells back, Engine 216 , " TURNOUT " It's a special building box at Pfizer Chemical Co.

We all turned out and climbed on to the Engine, Ron and I opened the firehouse doors and closed them as soon as the engine cleared the doors and jumped on the rear of the engine. Ron and Tony were riding the back step with me. And John Cass was up front in the jumpseat. My heart was beating double time. Ron yells out to me as the engine is screaming down Broadway Ave.(Brooklyn) towards Pfizer Chemical, "Looks like your first one is going to be a big one Andy."

I looked out to the side of the Engine as we approached the location, and I see the building coming up on the right . And I notice what looks like smoke coming out most of the windows, but it isn't pushing or black as usual.

The Engine pulls up in front of the building, and I'm ready to pull off a loop of hose with the nozzle , I'm all set to go into the building. But the other guys and the Lou (Lieutenant) are very casual and gather around me . I said to myself " what in the hell is wrong with these guys there's a fire going on.

Suddenly, they all start bending over laughing. And I said what's wrong". The Lou said with a chuckle ," Andy take a good look at the windows on the building, what you see isn't smoke, it's steam coming out of the windows, and this is normal for this building. And with laughter, "We knew you would think it was a fire, and we anticipated your reaction ". Don't worry you'll get your first one soon enough.

Let's go into the building and check it out. We went in and checked out the building And found out that the alarm tripped prematurely. It was a false alarm .

We all got back onto the rig and headed back to the house. On the way back we stopped at the grocery store to get what we needed for lunch. Today we will have knockwurst and sauerkraut.

We had just finished our lunch when we hear two fast rings on the house watch phone . Tony who took over house watch duties yells, Engine 216 turn out. Then the alarm comes in. We are first due at a fire at Lee Ave. and Hayward St.

My heart is jumping out of my chest with anticipation of my first fire. We all mount the Engine except for Tony and I who have to shut the house doors. The Engine pulls out and waits for Tony and I to jump on. The Engine heads down to Hayward St. We can smell the smoke as we approached the location . I look to the sky and can see the superheated smoke pushing skyward as we get closer to the scene of the fire. We are now on Hayward St. and the building is fully involved with fire. 108 Truck was just behind us. We pulled up to a hydrant close to the fire, Ron and I jumped off and grabbed the suction hose off the rig and wrapped it around the hydrant , we yelled to Phil , Take off", Phil took off with the engine to the other side of the fire building so that 108 Truck could place it's rig in front of the building .

Ron and I attached the suction hose to the hydrant, we then ran down to the Engine and joined the rest of the brothers with stretching the line, while Phil fastened the suction hose into the pumper . The building on fire was a two story vacant taxpayer (a building with a business on the ground floor and an apartment on top) . Lt. Mundi yelled over to me and told me to stick with him., so I was handed the nozzle, with Tony and the rest of the guys backing me up. We all crouched down low and got ready to move in on the fire. 108 truck was on the scene and started with the rear and roof ventilation. The front of the building was already ventilated by the fire and all the Engine Co. had to do was move in on the fire.

The Lou yells out OK , lets move in, I open up the nozzle and started moving in on the fire. The pressure from the nozzle was great . Tony backed me up on the nozzle, with Ron and John Cass moving the line in with us. Lt. Munda was up with me and Tony directing the attack on the fire.

We moved in on the fire, hitting the inferno with a solid stream and then with a circular motion so that the water could cool down the fire. The fire turned into steam as we moved into the into the building. And it's the steam that helps to cool down the fire and suffocate it. As the fire started to cool down I opened the S.O.S nozzle to a fog stream . This was very effective in cooling down the fire.

The smoke condition wasn't too bad because the building was well vented . As we moved in I could feel the plaster on the ceiling falling on us and deflecting off our helmets . The smoke was irritating my eyes and nose , as we moved in on it.

I could feel the fire radiating on me as it roared in front of us. The fire was starting to darken down as we moved in on it.. I noticed the fire blowing up the stairway ahead of us, and up to the second floor. The Lou yelled out, "Let's hit the stairway with water, Engine 237 has stretched a line in back of us and will take care of the second floor, as we finish knocking down the fire on the first floor ."

We started hitting the stairway with a stream of water, knocking down the fire so that Engine 237 could get into position as we moved into the fire at the rear of the first floor.

108 truck was ventilating the roof, relieving the heat and smoke from the building.

A lot of steam and white smoke was left as we finished off the last body of fire.

After 108 truck finished ventilating the roof they joined us in the interior to look for hot spots by pulling the ceiling to expose the rafters. When we spotted hot spots we washed them down.

With the fire out, the cold set in and the water was starting to freeze around us.

Engine 237 started to take up its line when they were done, and only the first due

Fire companies remained to finish up, which was the usual procedure. First to come last to go. As we started to take up our hose the Lou and the rest of the guys gave me a pat on the back and said I did good. That made my day. Lt. Mundi said it was the perfect fire for you to get your baptism with. It will help prepare you for the real bad ones to come. And they will come.

I broke out my rubber-insulated gloves with inserts to keep my hands warm while we loaded the hose on the Engine. I couldn't wait to get back to our warm firehouse and have a cup of coffee.

My thoughts went back to the bad fire that I missed. How cold it must have been that night in sub- freezing weather and searching for the victims of the fire.

I remember the Lieutenant with the patch over his eye at Proby School, when he told us recruits " Most of us will get injured 2 or 3 times before we get twenty years in, some seriously and one or two of us may die." It was a sobering thought.

After loading our hose back on the engine we headed back for home. We arrived at quarters and had a covering company waiting for us to return. They were very anxious for us to relieve them, they were from a quieter neighborhood and wanted to get back to their quarters as soon as possible.

After we had some coffee some of us went up to the bunk room to get some rest, just in case another alarm came in and a possible worker (fire)

It was my turn for my first house watch duty and I sure was apprehensive about screwing up on my first house watch duties.

Somebody knocks on the door I and take a look. Standing outside the door is a young lad who introduces himself as an auxiliary fireman. He said to me "You're new aren't you?" I said your right, I'm the new Proby with the company, My name is Andy, and what's your name? "My name is Leroy", Ok Leroy, shaking his hand come on in. I announced to Lt. Munda that Leroy the Auxiliary was in quarters .

Lt. Munda said , Leroy is OK. I thought to myself , I wasn't aware that there were auxiliaries working as volunteers in firehouses. It's a good way for young men who are interested in the job to become out future firefighters.

When we responded to fires, Leroy was helpful out side, helping us to stretch lines and also helping the chauffer of the engine. And when it was time to take up, Leroy would help us loading the hose on the bed of the engine.

Tony came to the house watch desk to talk to me ," I've got to show you how to maintain the coal stove in the basement." This was a new experience for me, most homes and apartment buildings had either oil, or gas heat these days, and I remember that a lot of multiple dwellings still use coal, remembering all the cans of cinders I carried and dumped in the garbage truck when I worked as a San man.

Tony showed me the coal furnace, and the importance of keeping enough water in the line by keeping an eye on the tube filled with water by the stove attached to the water line. He also showed me the bin full off coal and a shovel. It was the house watches duty especially on the night shift to make sure we had a fire going all the time.

47

The basement had a long narrow passageway. Tony said, "This passage way is perfect for me to practice my archery, I like to go bow hunting, and it keeps me in shape. "Hey I said back, I'm also a bow hunter. No kidding Tony said, we 've got to get together next hunting season. You've got it, it's a date. I know a couple of good spots up by Liberty New York. Tony and I were hitting it off good. Tony and

I would turn out to be good friends in the future.

When Tony and I got back upstairs, Leroy was sitting at the house watch desk and thumbing through the special building box response cards. Tony and I walked back to the kitchen for a cup of coffee, some of the brothers were sitting around and gabbing and drinking coffee. I mentioned that Leroy is really interested in the job, isn't he? Ron answered. "Yeah , he's kind of helpful around quarters."

APRIL 1968

It was now April and the weather was getting milder, this allowed the people to come outside, and hang around the streets. The good thing about the winter months was that the people remained in their houses and apartments, especially the teenagers , this kept the gangs off the streets. Now the scenario is starting to change, and the alarms are on the increase, at this time of the year it starts picking up momentum, especially after school hours. Automobile fires, rubbish fires, and vacant building fires start to plague us. This was just the beginning.

Today was April 4, and events in the City changed drastically, news flashed all over the media, Martin Luther King was assassinated. Riots and insurrection break out around the country and New York City was on top of the list. This is all we needed,

It was bad enough with the anti-war demonstrators.

A time bomb was ticking off in the city, especially in black neighborhoods.

More and more alarms were coming in, more and more automobiles are being stolen and torched , more and more vacant and occupied buildings are arsoned putting the lives of civilians and firefighters in jeopardy.

Civilians going to work, and passing through rioting neighborhoods are being pulled out of their automobiles by roving gangs and beaten , some are shot and killed when they resist being robbed. Many vehicles have broken bottles jammed under their wheels at stop lights, giving them blowouts thus forcing the inhabitants to abandon their vehicles which are stripped and torched. A lot of these people are mugged and beaten as they try to get to safety.

Some black people try to protect these people at their own peril.

More and more stories of firefighters getting seriously injured in booby trapped buildings start surfacing. In vacant buildings, floors are cut out just inside the apartments that are torched and covered with a carpet, and as the brothers are making the attack on the fire they fall through the floors into a fire that is deliberately set in an apartment on the floor below. Firefighters who are trained to save lives and property, are killed and seriously injured.

Bricks and Molotov cocktails are thrown off the roofs at firefighters and policeman who respond to fires.

When I get home after my tour of duty, I could see the worry on my wife's face, she knows when I'm at a fire, because of the aroma of smoke in my hair and body.

She relates to me about the news she hears on television.

"How did it go hon, were you very busy? " Yes, I answered back . "About the same as most days. How did it go for you today? I tried to keep it low keyed because I

51

didn't want her and the children to be worried . If I told her what was really going on she would be a nervous wreck while I was on tour.

I answered Chris " It wasn't too bad today, a few rubbish fires, car fires and an all hands at some vacant building a couple of blocks from the fire house.

Most of the teenagers are still in school yet, wait till school is out for the summer time, then all hell will break loose. It's bad enough after school hours"

"Where are the kids?" Chris answered they're with my Mom and Dad , should be back any minute, they went to the mall.

Chris approached me with a concerned look on her face, " Andy, I heard a firefighter was killed when he fell through a floor that was deliberately booby trapped. Is it true, Andy?

"Yes it's true I replied, don't worry hon., we're very careful, we check the floor in front of us before we move in on fire.

I'm fortunate to have a great bunch of men to work with, it's like a family away from home, and we also have some great cooks.

My wife Chris is a petite lady with Irish and Italian in her blood, when she's angry, the Irish comes out, when she cooks, the Italian comes out. Her Grandmother was Irish and her Grandfather was Italian. They both met when they came off the boat. They both opened up a restaurant in Coney Island, and passed off there cooking skills to my wife's Mom.

My background is the same as my wife's except, that I have Welsh , Scotch, Dutch and American Indian. My Great -grand mother on my Fathers side was full blooded Osage

Indian. I'm a real bonafide Heinz Variety all American Boy.

After the civil war my Great-grandfather traveled out west by covered wagon and settled in Flagstaff Arizona with a herd of sheep and some cattle. My grandfather Andy later on became a roundup boss for an Indian agency. It's amazing that I ended up a firefighter in Brooklyn N.Y., I should be out west, out on some range herding cattle.

The next day I have to work a night tour of duty. On my way to work, I take the long way. Instead of driving straight across Brooklyn ,from Flatbush to Williamsburg. I'll take the Belt Parkway around and into the Brooklyn Queens Expressway to avoid going through neighborhoods of high incidents of trouble. It was safer this way. I couldn't believe I had to do something like this to stay safe in my own town. On the way to work, looking out from the highway I could see columns of smoke pushing skyward from different locations in Brooklyn. I said to myself, the brothers are busy as usual.

I arrived for my day tour about half an hour before my tour began. Enough time to sit down and have some coffee.

Today I'd be working with the Capt. Scheer, Phil the Greek, Tony Amito, John Rossi ,Ron Hinks and Joe Cass.

The Captain said, " Today we have to catch up with some inspection duties. I'd like to go over to that factory on Union Ave and see if the owner moved those sewing machines away from the exit. That exit is the only way out for those ladies working in that sweat shop if the entrance is cut off. You know what factory I'm talking about , " Right Guys ". Yea , John Rossi said out loud, "You mean halitosis Harry. One breath from him and he'd knock us out for a week."

As we were heading to the sweatshop to check the place out, an alarm comes in for a rubbish fire at South 3rd and Hooper Street .

When we arrived at the the location of the fire, some people standing out side the front of the building told us that the fire was in the rear courtyard. We pulled the booster hose from the reel and headed for the courtyard in the rear of the building. 108 truck pulled up by us, and they joined us in the rear of the building. When we got back to the fire the stink of the garbage was over whelming. The garbage was knee deep in the courtyard and on fire. As we approached the fire, we could see rats scurrying away on the far side of the garbage heap. We all looked in disbelief. I thought that I was a Sanitation man at the garbage landfill again. The people just opened their windows and threw the garbage out of the windows into the courtyard. I guess they got tired of the smell and the rats, and decided to burn the garbage.

As John Cass knocked down the fire with the booster hose, the rest of us moved the garbage around with the hooks, to get at the hot spots. Sullivan, one of the brothers from 108, had a hook and was pushing and turning the heap of garbage when suddenly he gets belted with a bag of garbage that almost knocked off his helmet. " "What the hell , Jack say's, and yells up to the windows above. You filthy son of a ———. I'd like to shove this hook——— It was appalling , but we all broke out laughing looking at Sully with the garbage on his shoulders, and his helmet cocked to the side .

The Capt. and Lt. Zerch of 108 decided that we did our job, " Lets get out of this dump" they both motioned.

57

Andrew Ashurst

My brother Don was a Sanitation man in this district, when I see him I've got to tell him that half the garbage in Williamsburg is in the backyards.

108 truck left, and headed back to Siegal Street. Capt. Sheer told the Phil the Greek who was our chauffer for the tour, to stop at the grocery store so that we can get some food for lunch.

After this episode the thought of food kind of churned my stomach.

When we got back to quarters, the Greek fixed up some ham and cheese sandwiches for us, and we put a pot of coffee on.

After lunch the company turned out to go on an inspection tour of our district.

The Capt. told the Greek to head down Union Ave , " I want to check out that sewing machine place near Ten Eyck St. John Cass, Tony Amito and I were hanging on the back step when we started down Union Ave. As I looked down the sidewalk ahead of us I saw a head bobbing up and down. I knew the person, cause I recognized the hat on his head And the long black coat. It was attire that Hasidic Jews wear. The hat was big and round with fur trimmed around it on the brim and the person had black boots on.

I yelled to the guys. " Look that's the owner of the sweatshop ." Ron Hinks was up front by the Phil who was out chauffer, and yelled to Phil, " There's the owner of the sweat shop", Let's beat him to the factory, and check out the exit doors to see if he complied with the warning. The Capt. said " Good idea". Phil throttled up on the accelerator and started moving faster. The owner of the shop turned as he was walking and spotted us coming, and picked up the pace. We started to move faster knowing he was on to us. The shop owner excited, started to pick up the pace faster and started to jog. We were along side him now and started

59

to wave to him. " Hi Abby , what's the hurry? Abby waves back to us. Now he is at full gallop, running towards the shop to try to beat us to the factory. Phil takes off and leaves him behind a hundred yards.

The engine pulls up in front of the factory and we all bail out, except for the Greek who stayed with the rig. We scramble up the wooden stairs and into the factory. The women in the factory gives us smiles and giggles as we dashed to the rear exit. Sure enough , the exit was blocked again as usual, with sewing machines.

I said " This guy doesn't give a crap about the safety of these women working here." The Capt. said," We got to get this guy into court." No more Mr. Nice Guy."

Abby hurried into the factory, huffing and puffing, his face red as a peach. He knew we had him cold this time. The Capt. took him aside and read him the riot act. And handed him the summons. Tony Amito said, Hey Abby , you're fast on your feet. John Cass answered with a grin;"

Not fast enough".

"THE ATTACK ON FORT WILLIAMSBURG "

It's a steaming July day and we just finished having lunch . Most of the brothers were trying to get some rest upstairs in the bunk room after having a working fire this morning. We have no air conditioner and had the fans churning like B29s to get some air moving around. Lt. Mundi was down having some coffee and chatting with Charlie Benni our chauffer . .

The phone rings and Frank O'Malley who is on housewatch answers the phone.

"Hey Lou" O'Malley yells out. "Its 108 truck , they want you on the phone. Ok, Lt. Mundi answers I'll be right there. The Lou gets on the phone, " How's it going?" Yeh. huh , huh, no kidding, "You got it, see you later.

"Hey guys listen up, 108 was returning from a box and saw a group of men torching an automobile around the corner from us, on Meserole St. . We should be getting a call for a car fire soon. As soon as the alarm comes in the Engine and Truck will respond and put out the fire. After the fire is out , 108 Truck said they will go around the corner and wait for the people to disburse and then arrest and take in custody a couple of men who were involved.

In five minutes the alarm came in for the car fire. We turned out and responded around the corner. Sure enough there was the automobile, fully involved with fire.

There was at least twenty people in the streets yelling, shouting at us with obscene words and gestures. We put out the fire and went back to quarters and waited for 108 truck to contact us.

I went back upstairs to take a break. I was lying on the bunk bed, in anticipation to what was going on with 108 truck.

Suddenly I hear a roar out side quarters I ran to the front window and there's 108 Truck completely surrounded by people. The brothers from 108 yelled out, Engine 216 open the doors. I could see that they had two guys by the collar on the turn table of the ladder. The window was open, and I'll yelled down to them , we'll get you in. And they yelled back , " Hurry Up".

Every body in quarters turned to, we had a problem. If we open the doors all those people will invade the firehouse and attack us.

Tony yells out " I know how we can do this! I've got the bow and some arrows in my locker. When you open the door, I'll scare the people back with the bow and arrow. This will give the guys on the Truck time enough to get in and shut the door. Lt. Mundi , thought for a second, it may work. OK let's do it. So Toni Amito takes off up the stairs to get his bow and arrows out of the locker, and is back in a flash. . Lt. Mundi yells out, "OK, are you guys ready? Let's go.

Joe Cass and John Rossi got on each door and rolled them back as fast as possible. The doors are open and the crowd outside was trying to make a move on us. But Tony held the people at bay with the bow and arrow. It worked perfectly. The brothers on the Truck ran in as fast as possible, leaving the mob and the culprits behind. The Truck was at the mercy of the mob outside.

Meanwhile we called for police support.

Suddenly we heard rocks smashing through the upstairs windows and bouncing on the bunk room floors.

We all went back to the kitchen area to plan our strategy , when Charlie Benni notices out of the back window, men coming from an alleyway on the next street to get to the rear of our quarters . They started climbing the fence in our back yard.

Charlie yells out, "We're being attacked from the rear."

I'm going to start up the Engine and get the booster hose going. Lt. Mundi yells out ,Yea, Get the hose upstairs guys so that we can stop them from coming up the fireescape. Mean while The guys in the Engine donned their turnout clothing and helmits for protection. The men from 108 had their tools with them . Axes, Hooks, Haligan tools. And the members of 216 grabbed tools off the Engine in case there is hand to hand combat. We looked like Knights in a Crusade ready to do battle. There had to be at least a hundred people out side attacking our quarters.

Charlie got the Engine started and the water flowing to the booster hose just in time. The invaders started climbing to the fire escape, and we opened up with the water, knocking them off as they tried to get on the fire escape and enter the rear door. Lt. Foley of 108 truck yells out " I hope the hell the cops get here before the booster tank empties. "

What's keeping them?

Suddenly in a distance we heard the sirens blaring, and so did the invaders. They started to leave the scene real fast so they wouldn't be trapped like rats in the back yard with no way out.

New York's Finest came in force to the rescue . It sounded almost like the Calvary coming, with the bugles blowing. There were police cars all over the place. We asked what kept them from responding sooner ? They said that they were in involved with mob violence in other parts of the district. It was a close call, if we had got involved with hand to hand combat, blood would have spilled.

I guess in a sense , we put out another fire, with a hose and water.

When the police came on the scene we went out to to the front of quarters to see if there was any damage to 108 truck. The brothers of 108 truck reported that the truck was stripped clean of all its tools and equipment, except for the tools they had on them to protect themselves. Luckily we didn't have any calls to fires while this incident happened. There would have been a delay in response and lives could have been jeopardized. And 108 truck would have to respond without power tools and other vital tools. That's if they would have been able to get to the truck, without being attacked by the mob. The quarters of Engine 216 would have been ransacked and would have been at the mercy of the mob.

When the night shift guys came on duty, we told them what happened. They said strange, there wasn't any news in the media about the incident.

Tony Amito grabbed one of his arrows and jammed it into the canopy covering the Engine hose bed. There happened to be a burn mark on the canopy were Tony stuck the arrow, from a fire that we were at a while ago. Every body started laughing. I yelled out " This looks like my ancestors covered wagon after an Indian attack "

When I got home that evening I told Chris the story, and asked if she heard anything on the media. She said no, and had the T.V on all day. The next day , nothing in the media. The whole event never made the news.

The event was squashed like it never happened. It was hard to believe. This would have been a golden news item for the media.

Andrew Ashurst

"THE ENEMY WITHIN"

False Alarms, arsons and structural fires were on the increase. Abandoned auto fires rose to an all time high.

On the day shift and part of the evening shifts the Auxiliary Firefighters would give us a hand in the street stretching our lines and loading the hose after a fire was extinguished . We also had another Auxiliary that used to help us out, his name was Anthony. Him and Leroy were a lot of help.

Strange things started to occur while we responded to false alarm boxes. One day we responded to a box, and when we returned to quarters heard some noise in the back, by the kitchen. When we checked it out, the back door was open.

Somebody was in the firehouse. But nothing was taken. I guess we got back sooner than they expected. From then on we had to secure the place with better locks. Another time

we responded to one of our notorious false alarm boxes and

while I was on the back step of the Engine with John Cass,

somebody threw a brick at us. John and I could feel it wiz

by us. It was possible that somebody knew our response

areas and which way we traveled to them.

The incidents repeated themselves time and time again,

as someone would lie in wait for us to respond to the alarm

box and the missiles would fly. But whoever was throwing

the stuff at us couldn't hit the side of a barn. Thank God.

Then one day I had to go to the medical office down at

Spring St. in Manhattan.

When I got to the medical office. I noticed a familiar

face washing a chief's car out side the medical office. It was

Leroy, our auxiliary. I said to myself, what in the hell is he

doing over here. I yelled out to him to get his attention, so that I could be sure it was him. "Hey, Leroy how did you find your way over here? Oh aaa hi

Andy, I thought I would come over here and volunteer little. Puzzled , I said, "Sounds good". When I worked my next shift I told the guys about seeing Leroy over at the medical office. And they all had a surprise look on their faces.

The weeks went by and one night we got a call from one of the other Engine Companies in the Battalion and they said to us. " Guess what, Engine 216, we spotted your auxiliary Leroy walking in our neighborhood with a Lieutenant's uniform on. He took off when we spotted him and got away. We passed the info on to headquarters, so that they could look into it. I guess they want to watch his movements for a while. We all looked at each other, and the light bulbs started to go on in our heads. Yea, he did spend a lot of his time looking into our response cards didn't he!

And Andy spotted him over at the medical office a few weeks ago. I wonder if he was involved with the false alarms, and arsons going on in the neighborhood, and also the bricks being thrown at us. Iwonder what other places he hangs out within the Dept.?

THE ENEMY WITHIN CONTINUES

Its late in Sept. and John Flanagan and Shawn Collins of the Fire Marshal's office were detailed to follow Leroy, and to see if he may be involved with any group or groups that were involved with harassing firefighters, arson and activating false alarms.

They arrived about 5:00 in the evening near Leroy's residence in an unmarked van, hoping he would lead them to others that may be involved with breaking thelaw. They could have arrested him for impersonating an officer, but were going for higher stakes. It was good timing, because they spotted Leroy coming up the block and then enter his residence.

Flanagan says to Collins. " Now we know that he is home, he probably came home to eat supper. With any luck he'll leave after he eats and show us the way to his hangout. And with any luck we can catch them red handed.

I hope nobody gets wise to this van, and our cover isn't blown.

Flanagan and Collins opened up a brown bag to take out some coffee and sandwiches anticipating a watch for a couple of hours.

Both men were active in fire companies once, and decided to become fire marshals after 10 or so years on the job . It was a change in pace, involving arson investigation and internal problems.

It was about 7:00 P.M and Leroy didn't come out of the house yet. Both Flanagan and Collins thought maybe they pic ked a bad night. But tonight was a good night, it was warm out, a clear sky. It was a good night for activity.

The kids started to come out of their houses and mill around the front steps of the house" I guess dinner is over, said Flanagan." Yea, Shawn replied, this could be bad. They'll get curious and we'll have to beat it.

Suddenly, out the door comes Leroy, luckily he walks away from where the van is parked, and starts up the street. Half way down the block he crosses the street and continues walking to the corner. When he gets to the corner, he goes right and disappears . Flanagan and Collins get the van sta rted and drive to thecorner and spot Leroy talking to a group of teenage boys outside a luncheonette.

John and Shawn noticed they were carrying brown paper bags with them.

So they wouldn't be suspicious they drove the van past the group and went to the next corner and pulled up in front of a bakery shop. Shawn jumps out of the van and tells John to keep an eye on them and I'll go in and buy some doughnuts. While

Shawn was getting some doughnuts the group of teenage boys started to walk down on the opposite side of the street. John waves to Shawn inside the bakery, motioning to hurry up. Shawn comes hurrying out with a bag of doughnuts and jumps into the van. Where did they go? They came back down the street and disappeared around the corner in back of us. I hope we spot them when we get to the corner. Flanagan drives to the corner and makes a U- turn and heads for the intersection where the gang was last seen. Flanagan approaches the intersection with ease to see if he can spot the group of boys . Sure enough they are spotted about half way up the block. Flanagan pulls into a spot behind a car. We can spot them from here, as long as they go straight. It looks like they're headed for Bushwick Ave and if that's were they're going , I've got a good idea what they're up to. Collins replies, "Do you think they're headed for the vacant building on Bushwick and Mckibbin ?

That's what I'm hoping , if so, maybe we'll catch them in the act of arson.

We had better move up closer, they're starting to walk out of sight. With this Flanagan moves the van from its spot and slowly moves up closer to the group walking up ahead, " I think I'll grab this space up ahead. " We can watch them from here until it's time for us to get closer. Meanwhile let's have a couple of doughnuts.

Leroy and the gang had paper bags with bottles full of gasoline, and were anxious to start a fire in one of the vacant buildings near Bushwick Ave.

Leroy says to his cohorts. " The building is up ahead guys, let's try to enter without anybody noticing us, But I think the best thing to do is, all of us go and have some coffee someplace near by, and wait for it to get a little darker out." His friends agreed. There's a place to have coffee about a block away from the building.

We'll go there and kill some time.

Flanagan and Collins watched the group as they walk past Bushwick Ave and up another block then disappear into a building . Collins with surprise said,

"I thought for sure they would go into that vacant building," Flaherty answered.

"I had the same thoughts," We had better get up to the next street and see if we can spot them"! Flanagan pulls the van out of its parking space and drives the vanto where they saw the gang disappear into a building . "Ah" Collins says here's where they went, into the luncheonette . Don't look inside, we'll just casually driveby

"I wonder what they're up to, Flanagan ponders.? We have to find a place to park near the luncheonette without being noticed or drawing suspicion. Who knows how long they'll be inside. We may as well finish our doughnuts for now.

Flanagan and Collins decided to go up another block ,
make a U-Turn and come back down the street where the
luncheonette was located and look for a parking place not to
far from the luncheonette . Maybe I'll go in and get us some
java, Collins tells Flanagan then replies, " No, I don't think
that's a good idea." We're kind of out of our environment
her e, and they may get suspicious of you, especially
withthose plain black shoes that you're wearing. Shawn
answers." You're right, why take a chance. If they got on to
us, it could jeopardize the whole investigation.

It's close to 8:00 P.M. and it's starting to get dark out
when, Flanagan and Collins notice Leroy and his friends exi
t the luncheonette and head back to the vacant tenement
building.

Looks like we're not going to be disappointed Shawn,
They' re heading towards the vacant building. We'll wait

until they enter the building and then call the 90 Precinct for some back up. Let's hope we catch them in the act of arson.

Leroy and his gang entered the vacant tenement building. And Flanagan and Collins waited about 5 minutes for the 90 to arrive on the scene.

A plain car with detectives showed up and parked by the building out of site, with a regular patrol car around the corner waiting to be called to the scene.

Flanagan, Collins I. D. themselves to the detectives and told them what the score was. They then entered the building as quiet as possible, O.K , Flanagan whispers, we have to wait until they try setting a fire. Then we'll nail them.

Leroy and the gang were up on the third floor and cutting a hole in the floor just beyond the entrance of the apartment. After that was done they started spreading the gasoline throughout the rooms . O.K guys let's get out of here, and on the way down we'll spill the rest of the gas in the apartment below and then on the stairs before we light up the place. Leroy said, " Maybe we'll roast a fireman tonight".

Hiding inside a doorway of an apartment on the first floor, Flanagan ,Collins and the detectives heard every word that was said, and waited in anticipation for them to head down the stairs.

Suddenly the gang started moving down the stairs and spilling gasoline on their way down. They were now on the first floor and Leroy took out a book of matches and got ready to ignite the gasoline.

Flanagan told the detectives "OK Now" . And with that, they jumped out of the doorway with their guns drawn, yelling to the gang, " Don't move, You're all under arrest." One of the detectives alerted the patrol car, and they were on the scene in seconds.

Leroy cries out. " We didn't do nothing , why are we being arrested? Shawn answers him back. "I tell you what Leroy, why don't you and your friends go back upstairs and I'll light up a cigarette. And then you'll know why you're all under arrest, while you're all roasting in the fire .

The police handcuffed them and read them their rights, and waited for the patty wagon to arrive.

Flanagan called up the Brooklyn Fire Department Dispatcher to send an Engine Co. over to the scene, to wash down the gasoline on the floors above, and the stairways.

Shawn said, " Thank God we nailed these guys tonight, it could have been a tragedy for our brothers fighting this fire. Especially with the hole cut out on the third floor. Later on it was found out that Leroy and his gang were involved with setting numerous fires in the area , and were connected to a larger organization involved with arson and setting booby traps in the buildings to injure firefighters

MEAT LOAF FOR DINNER

Another night shift is about to begin . The men line up for role call. The men working tonight are Lt. Munda, John Rossi, our chauffer for the night, Gus Landi, Ron Hinks, Frank O'Malley, and myself.

Roll call is over and John walks over to the kitchen, turns around and then yells out to us all . Who's in on the meal ? Everybody in turn yells back, that they're in.

Lt. Munda say's "We should get an alarm soon, a false alarm usually comes in about this time. And we can stop by the grocers and get a meal.

Sure enough an alarm comes in, and its one of our notorious false alarm box's. Ron Hinks who is on first watch, yell's out , "216 turn out."

John ask's Ron, "Where are we going ?" Ron yells back, Bushwick Ave. and Meserole Streets. Ron and I open the doors to the apparatus floor and John drives the Engine out of quarters with a blast from the Engine's air horn and siren. Lt. Munda is up front with John . Gus and Frank are in the jump seats behind John and the Lou.

As soon as the Engine clears the doors Ron and I push the doors closed and jump on the rear of the Engine.

John Rossi makes a right to Union Ave. Then makes a left on Union and heads down to Meserole Street with the sirens and air horn blasting. At Meserole we make another left and head for Flushing Ave.

Ron and I are hanging on the rear of the Engine looking skyward to see if there is any smoke pushing into the sky , a certain sign that we have a working fire. I yell over to Ron, " Ron do you see anything on your side"? " No " He yells back.

Nothing"

The Engine started to slow down as we approached the intersection of Bushwick and Meserole. No sign of fire or smoke . The Engine stopped at the intersection And we jumped off the rig and made a search spreading out down the intersection north , east , west and south . Ron and I split up, I went north, Ron went south, Gus went east and Frank went west. We all ran down about a half a block a piece searching the area as we ran down. Nothing was seen and no civilians calling us for help. It looked like another false alarm.

After the search we all returned to the box. Lt. Munda was at the box and rewinding the mechanism so that the box will be set again.

The Lou, yells out." O.K guys let's go to the super market and get some food for tonight."

When the Company arrived at the neighborhood super market we all decided on meat loaf, mashed potatoes and vegetables.

John gave us the list of food to get, and we did the shopping. John and the Lou remained with the Engine in case an alarm came in.

It only took us 10 minutes to get what we needed and headed back to the firehouse.

John was our cook for the night and always made a good meal for us all.

Ron continued on with house watch duties as Frank, Gus and I peeled the potatoes and prepared them for the meal.

In about an hour the meal was ready .John yelled out , " It's on the table, come and get it."

The aroma of the meat loaf and mashed potatoes, and especially the heated dinner rolls, started to water my mouth. We were all as hungry lions, and couldn't wait to dig in.

We all sat down and got ready to eat, I sliced a piece of meat loaf and got ready to eat it when the phone gave out 3 quick rings . Almost all together we all yelled out No, No, What the hell. Ron was on his way to the kitchen and ran back to the house watch desk to answer the phone. Ron answered the phone and yelled back to us, " Engine 216 TURN OUT ". We have a worker at Lee and Hayward Sts.

We all dropped our eating utensils and ran to the Engine and donned our turn out gear. Ron was ready to go and opened the apparatus floor doors . Before I left the kitchen I grabbed a roll and shoved it in my mouth.

The Engine with it sirens and air horn blasting, headed for Union Ave. made a left and headed for Hayward St. We could see the heavy black smoke pushing skyward as we headed down Union Ave. As we got closer, burning red embers could be seen blended in with the superheated black smoke as it pushed into the sky. Ron and I snapped in our clips on the upper end of our turn out coats and turned up our collars as we approached the fire.

We could see the fire blowing out of a vented front window, on the third floor, of a four story walk up apartment building.

John pulled the Engine up in front of the building and stopped . Ron and I pulled off three loops of hose a piece as Frank and Gus also joined us pulling off three loops of hose . This would be enough for the stretch to the third floor.

Lt. Mundi jumped out of the rig and joined us. The Lou yelled to John. " John take off.

John gave some throttle to the Engine and took off to a hydrant about twenty feet away. About this time 108 Truck was on the scene .

Lt. Mundi , Dal, Frank ,Gus and I stretched to the doorway as Gus dropped the last length of hose on the floor in the hall way and ran to the Engine to help John hook up to the Engine.

The forceable entry team of 108 truck joined us as we started to stretch up the stair way to the fire floor .

We could hear the other fire companies arriving at the scene . Ladder 109, Engine 230 and Engine 211 were also on the first alarm assignment.

Gus finished helping John hook up and donned a Scott Pack and Mask and straightened the line out in the street to make sure there were no kinks in the line .

While he was doing this we were ready to enter the apartment.

Lt. Mundi yelled to John over his handy talkie to start water. I opened the nozzle to allow the air in the line to escape as line was charged and the water was racing up to us. I shut down the nozzle momentarily as two members of 108 truck forced the door open. We were all crouched down as low as possible. As soon as the door was forced open the members of 108 Truck moved to the side, and I opened up the nozzle with a blast of water . We started moving in on the fire, Dal was my back up and helped me move in, because the nozzle was under high pressure. Lt. Mundi was right with us giving us a helping hand as we moved in. The other members of 108 Truck were ventilating the rear windows and the skylight on the top floor hallway as we started to move in .The smoke was burning my eyes and I started tearing, the tears coated my eyes and this made it possible to see better, and also stop most of the irritation from the smoke . After about three minutes of taking a beating . I felt a tap on the shoulder, it was Gus with the Scott pack and mask yelling to me to take a break. Gus took over the nozzle and Frank relieved Ron as the back up man as Ron and I took our places in back of Frank and Gus moving the heavy line in as the fire was knocked down . We moved in slowly from one room to another from one room to another.

The fire was darkening down and the members of 108 truck entered the apartment for a search of victims.

We knocked down the fire in all the rooms. The guys from 108 said the apartment was searched, and nobody was at home. Thank God. The chief came on the scene, looked around and told us we did a good job and said we can take up as soon as we finished overhauling . After we were sure that all the hot spots were extinguished, after all the hot spots were taken care of, Lt. Mundi said, "OK guy's were done here. " Lets take up the hose and get back to the meat loaf.

After placing the hose on the rig, Lt. Mundi walked over to the alarm box about twenty feet away and re-set the alarm box. We all jumped on the rig and headed back for home.

We got back to the firehouse and opened the doors, and held back the traffic as John backed the Engine into quarters. As soon as the engine was in quarters we all headed for the kitchen to finish our meal . John put the oven on so that we could heat the food up real quick (We had no Microwaves in them day's).

After the food was heated up we all sat down to eat.

We were starved, and began to eat. No sooner then we had two mouth fulls of food. Another alarm comes in . Frank O'Malley took over house watch duties at this time and yells back," We have a relocation assignment in Brownsville (a section of Brooklyn) to Engine 236 .

Ron yells out. "I can't believe it," "I can't believe it", I'm dying of hunger. We all shook our heads . John yells out , " We'll take the food with us " . So we grabbed a pan and put the meat loaf in the pan and another vessel for the mashed potatoes and vegetables. We threw the roles in a bag real quick and loaded the food on the hose bed of the Engine. We all donned our Turnout Gear and got ready to go .

Frank and Ron opened up the doors and out the Engine went, stopping for a moment so that Frank and Ron could shut the doors and jump on.

Engine 216 took off for Brownsville made a left on Union Ave. and into Broadway . Broadway would take us right into the Brownsville section of Brooklyn.

When we arrived at Engine 236 quarters we could see them operating at a fire about six blocks down from their quarters.

We jumped off the rig and held back the traffic as John backed the rig into quarters. As soon as the Engine was in quarters we got the food off the hose bed and brought it into the kitchen . We grabbed some dishes out of 236's kitchen cabinets and set the table real quick. John turned the oven on , so that we could have warm food. We put some coffee on, thanks to 236's commissary.

We all sat down except Frank O'Malley who was still on house watch duty.

Frank will have his food at house watch.

Gus said, " Looks like we'll be able to eat in peace now".

John dished out the food and we all began to dig in. Suddenly the bells start ringing . We didn't think anything of the bells because we weren't familiar with the alarm boxes in this area. Frank would count the bells and check 236's alarm box chart.

Suddenly Frank yells out, " ENGINE 216, TURN OUT "

NO, NO , NO, Gus and the rest of the men almost together like a quire yell out.

Will we ever eat this meal.

Frank quickly pulls out the alarm location card on file at the house watch desk and hands it to Lt. Mundi who will tell John the directions to the location.

We left the food on the table and donned our turn out gear . Everybody climbed on to the rig. I ran to the front doors and gave Frank a hand opening the doors.

John Rossi pulled the rig out and Frank and I closed the doors and jumped on the rig.

The alarm was about five blocks from quarters . It was a three story brownstone bldg. And the fire was on the top floor, judging by the smoke coming out of the top floor window. We pulled up to a hydrant by the building on fire. Some civilians in front of the building yelling said that the fire was in the apartment on the top floor. We stretched our line up the front stoop and into the building. When we got half way up, between the second floor and the top floor, smoke was pouring out of an open door , no fire was visible yet. Lt. Mundi called John Rossi over the handi- talkie and told him to start water. Ron was on the nozzle and opened the nozzle a bit to allow the air rushing through the hose to escape. We then moved in and saw the fire in what looked like the kitchen. We moved in on the fire with a fog pattern to cool the fire down . The fire was just starting to get under way. We knocked down the fire quickly as the Truck Company moved in to check it out.

"Looks like food on the stove guy's" One of the Truckee's yelled over to us.

They searched the apartment carefully to make sure the fire didn't extend to other parts of the apartment and also searched for possible victims.

Everything looked clear, so the Lou told us to take up the line. We dragged the line out to the street . The street was loaded with civilians, and also a couple of police cars to hold up traffic.

We disconnected the hose from the pumper and also disconnected the other lengths of hose. Each of the men grabbed a length of hose and drained the water out . We then loaded the hose one length at a time, folding each length neatly on the bed of the rig. When this was accomplished we all got on the rig . John drove the rig to the alarm box location so that Lt. Mundi could reset the alarm.

When this was done The Lou yelled out , "OK let's go and eat."

We got back to Engine 236's quarters only to find that Engine 236 had returned from their job. We looked at each other with disbelief and hungry stomachs.

The men from engine 236 gave us a warm greeting, as we entered their quarters to pick up the food. We told the members of 236 that we have been trying to eat this meal since 6:30 this evening.

We put the meat loaf in the pan that we took with us and put the vegetables in one of the pots that we had, and dumped the mashed potatoes.

We got on the Engine and headed back to our quarters. When we got back into quarters we took the food off the hose bed and set it on the kitchen table.

John Rossi yells out. "Any body for cold meatloaf sandwiches.

The rest of the night was uneventful.

ANOTHER MIRACLE

It was another hot day in Williamsburg Brooklyn. The thermometer read in the 90's. But the heat didn't bother Charlie Benni as he was lifting is weights in the Rec. room off the kitchen. He was doing a 300 lb. benchpress . Charlie was of medium height and strong like a bull. It was a toss up who Mr. America of the Firehouse was, Charlie, the Captain or another firefighter named Jimmy Morris.

"Com-mon Andy, give it a try Charlie yells over to me" sure I said , but not 300 lbs. I'll try 150. Sounds good Charlie replies.

I got up from the table and walked over to the bench and helped Charlie take off a 150 hundred lbs of weight. I then laid down on the bench and proceeded to lift the weights off the stand above me. Charlie was in back of me to assist just in case. I lifted the 150lbs up and down to my chest . I then

100

pro ceeded to push up with the weights and got about six inches away from my chest and that was it.

Charlie started to laugh and grabbed the bar with the weights and said. Not bad, not bad Andy, all you need is some training. If your interested I can help you get started. I don't know Charlie, I said . I like exercise better, like gymnastics and that kind of stuff. I use to do that in High School. Hey, that's OK, Charlie responded as long as you keep your self in shape.

Lt. Brown a covering officer was assigned to us today. He was just made Lt. And was still bouncing around, until he got himself his own company.

He was a quite type of a guy, and from a slower area. And wasn't familiar with the Williamsburg area of Brooklyn. We all reassured him that we'd help him out with the area, and that the men were seasoned firefighters and knew the Job.

When we told him this he looked more at ease. Thanks for the support fellas, he responded. Glad to help Lou, we chimed in.

A few alarms came in over the next couple of hours. Mostly rubbish fires, stolen vehicles set on fire and the usual false alarms.

Then an alarm comes in for a fire near Wycoff and Myrtle Ave's. We're first due on a second alarm, so we are standby just incase a second alarm comes in. But shortly after , Engine 216 is called out on a special call to that alarm. I guess they didn't need a full second alarm assignment at the location.

Engine 216 turns out to the location. Upon arrival at the scene we could see that the fire was a commercial building . There was fire on every floor. But not extensive. Most of the fire was on the street level floor.

The Chief in charge told us to stretch a line up a 35 ft. extension ladder to the second floor. Ron Hinks, Frank O'Malley take the 35 Ft. Extension ladder off the Engine while Tony Amito and I grabbed a couple of lengths of hose off the bed of the Engine . Ron and Frank placed the ladder against the wall to the window.

While I'm waiting to go up the ladder, I notice smoke pushing out of the mortar joints on the wall of the building. I yell out to the Lt. And call him over . The Lou steps over to me and say's " What's up Andy' ? I said to him " Look at the brick joints Lou, isn't that smoke pushing out a sign of a possible collapse?"

Yes, said the Lieutenant back to me. I'll let the Chief in charge know about the situation. I'll be right back. The Lieutenant walked over to the Chief in charge And told him about the situation. The Chief looked over briefly and said a few words .

The Lieutenant walked back to us and told us that the Chief wants us to go in.

So with that we all started up the ladder and into the building.

When we entered the floor we noticed that the floor area was clear and the fire was down at the left of us. Tony had the nozzle and we all helped stretching the line inside the second floor close to the fire. The Lou called Charlie to start water .

We had the fire knocked down in a few minutes. The Lieutenant asked me to take over the nozzle and vent the smoke out of the floor by the window.

Tony handed the nozzle over to me and we dragged the hose over to the window and I opened the S.O.S nozzle (Select O Stream) into a fog position and started To whip it around facing the open window. This started pulling the smoke out of the second floor. Frank and Ron stood back from me cause it was a one man operation.

After a while Frank and Ron called over to me, Andy shut down , take a break.

I shut down the hose and proceeded to walk in the direction of Frank and Ron.

It was dark on the floor, and the floor didn't feel right. When Ron and Frank approached me to take over I told them to be careful. I don't like the way the floor feels. The Lieutenant and Tony were on the other side of the floor with the truck company checking for hot spots with their flashlights to make sure the fire was out. No sooner than I told Ron and Frank to be careful I felt the floor underneath give one jerk downward. With that I jumped for the window, and the floor collapsed with a loud rumble a debris flying every where . I was hanging on the window with no floor under me.

I had my Scott pack on and my mask was clipped on my turn out coat and could I was holding on for dear life.

I turned and yelled down into the darkness below for Ron and Frank , with no response. I was afraid that they were hurt seriously or God forbid killed when they went down with the floor.

I managed to pull myself up to ledge of the window when I noticed a helmet coming up the ladder it said Rescue 2 on it. It sure was nice to see those guys on the scene. They got me out of the window and onto the ladder. As soon as I got down to the street floor, I looked for Ron and Frank. There they were, standing next to the Engine brushing their turnout clothes off. They got out without a scratch, it was a relief to see them uninjured. We were lucky once more. It was another miracle that nobody got hurt or worse, killed.

Author with family, Chief of Fire Dept. and Commissioner
During Medal Day Ceremonies

Engine 216 and members

Engine 216 and members

108 Truck Co. and Members

108 Ladder Co. and Engine 216
Operating at a fire.

Members of 216
Author kneeling up front

Members of Engine Co. 216

Engine 216 and Ladder 108 working at a fire.

Author Left

Johnny Carson at F.D.N.Y. Proby School

Chief Nemechek
35th Battalion

"VOILA"

It's November and it's starting to get chilly in the evenings. It's a night shift and 6:00 P.M and the company is mustering in. Lt.Mundi is briefing us, and the situation in the city doesn't look good as far as fires are concern. Fires are still on the increase, along with false alarms.

I have the house watch duties, and the bells didn't stop ringing, the circuits were open and companies were being turned out all over Brooklyn. Suddenly an alarm comes in for us." Box 239 , I yelled out,

Engine 216 turnout." the men on duty scrambled to their positions on the Engine while I opened the doors to quarters. The engine chauffeur Charlie Benni, pulled the Engine out with the sirens on. Frank O'Malley helped me close the doors and we both jumped on the rear of the Engine. The alarm box was only around the corner. We pulled up to the location and the brothers spread out down the across the intersection looking for any signs of fire. It looked clear, another false alarm, I said to myself.

Near the corner were a group young men, two of them looked our way with smirks on their faces. Lt. Mundi asked them if they had seen anyfbody pull the alarm.

They looked at each other with that dumb but not so dumb look, and one of them yelled back. " No, We didn't see nobody pull the alarm. "

Lt. Mundi answered them back. " You know, one of these days somebody is going to pull a false alarm and someone is going to die in a fire because we couldn't respond in time."

Lt. Munda said, " Ok guys let's get some chow while we are out of quarters.

John Rossi, one of our cooks yelled . " Who's in on the meal?"We all gave him our answers that we are in on the meal. We stopped at the supermarket while John and I went in to get the food. John picked out some chicken and potatoes etc. while I went to find some cake for dessert. It only took us about ten minutes to get what we needed. And we started back to quarters.

Lt. Mundi didn't have chance to put his car in the lot yet and parked a couple of spaces up from quarters. Charlie backed the engine into quarters and we all got off . Lt. Mundi headed for his car saying "

I better get this car in the lot before it disappears. " I remained at the housewatch desk to make an entry that we were back in quarters. Lt. Mundi returns upset. " The damned car won't start, it was ok when I parked it". I yelled back to one of the guys to listen out while I take a look at the Lou's car. Lt. Mundi opened the hood of his car. We couldn't believe our eyes, somebody took the battery out of the car. Lt. Mundi said "They had to do this while we were out of quarters. We were only gone about 15 minutes.

One of these days I'll catch the bums. I guess we'll have to stop at an auto supply place and pick up a battery for the car when we're out of quarters again."

It didn't take long and an alarm came in for a car fire. We responded to the car fire which was up on Humbolt Street. 108 truck was at the scene when we arrived. It was an abandoned automobile. We stretched the booster hose off the engine and knocked down the fire. We told the brothers of 108 about Lt. Mundi's battery being stolen out of his car they laughed a little, and one of the guys said " Isn't it a lovely neighborhood that we live in!

Dinner was ready, John Rossi, out did himself again. We all sat down and dug into the meal.

116

We ate our meal quickly because the alarms were coming rapidly, and it was only matter of time that one of alarm boxes would come in.

We had just finished our meal and an alarm came in. The alarm was on Manhatten and Lenord streets. When we arrived there was a man standing out side a building waiving and yelling over to us " "Over here, Over here"."

The civilian told us that there was smoke coming out of the door on the second floor. The members of 108 trucks forcible entry team ran up the stairs as we stretched a line behind them, and proceeded to make it up to the second floor doorway.

We got ready to move in, and Lt. Mundi gave the orders over the handy-talkie to Charlie to start water. The water was on its way up the hose as the members of 108 forced the locked door open.

When the door was forced opened, the smoke poured out. By the smell of the smoke it was obvious that it was a food on the stove fire. The fire ignited the wall in back of the stove.

Mullins of 108 truck was able to use the water can extinguisher to knock down the small body of fire. A search was done by the other members of 108, and they found a man sleeping on a couch in room by the kitchen. The brothers shook the guy and woke him up. " Hey guy", they said out loud. "You damned near slept for eternity."

We started taking up the hose, draining out the water and folding the hose back on the bed of the Engine. When we were done, Lt. Mundi made a call to the Brooklyn dispatcher and let the know that Engine 216 was back in service.

Within seconds Charlie yells back to us " We got another run " hang on.

John Rossi yells over to O'Malley and me; "It's a good thing we had our meal tonight, who knows how long we would be running tonight."

Charlie drives the Engine over to Broadway Ave. Makes a left and picking up speed races down Broadway with the Engines siren blaring.

O'Malley yells out to Ron Hinks, who is up front. " Ron, where are we going? " Ron yells back, We got a special call to Brownsville. John Rossi yelled out "A special call to Brownsville"!

What in the hell is going on in Brownsville, we're second due at a fire. Why would they to pull us out of our district when we're responding to a fire?

We have enough problems in Williamsburg to take care of, never the less Brownsville."

It was dark out, and I looked ahead up at the sky, the sky was lit up with a red glow, it seemed far away. As we got closer to area of response, the sky was lighting up like the Aurora Borealis with fire embers rising to the sky. O'Malley who was peering over at his side yelled out . It looks like London during the blitz.

As we pull into the area of response, John Rossi yells out " Voila ". There were at least three vacant multiple dwellings involved with fire. We couldn't get near the fire because of all the hose stretched by numerous Engine Co's.

The Super Pumper was in place with its diesel engines purring and supplying a large manifold lying out in the street, so that numerous Companies can hook up to the manifold to fight their individual fires. We could feel the heat of the fires radiating off us like a sauna, civilians were all over the place and New York's finest (NYPD)had their hands full. Lt. Mundi yelled over to us to grab folded lengths and carry them over to the manifold and hook up. We were ordered by the Chief to stretch a line to a vacant building across the intersection, and wash down the interior stairs, because somebody poured gasoline down the stairs.

We stretched the line to the door way of the building and pulled it into the hallway, The Chief was right, the odor of gasoline stunk up the place. All that was needed was a spark and the place would have lit up. Lt. Mundi called Charlie on the phone to start water. I was on the nozzle, and opened it slightly, to release the air pressure. When the line was charged,

I started to wash down the stairs in front of us. Rossi and O'Malley backed me up as I started to move up the stairs. Ron Hinks and Gus Landi moved the line in from the street as we moved in.

We were half way up the stairs washing it down when Lt. Mundi gets a call from Charlie," Lou, the sons of bitches are trying to cut our line, send a couple of guys out quick" Lt Mundi yelled down to Ron and Gus " Get out to Charlie, quick, somebody out there is trying to cut the line.

Ron and Gus were out the door in a second and saw Charlie running down from the manifold towards a teenager with a hatchet, getting ready to cut into the line. Ron and Gus took off after the individual yelling, get away from the line you son -of- a bitch. The kid sees them coming throws the hatchet down, and takes off, disappearing between two buildings. Charlie said " Let him go, we'll never catch him, we have enough on our hands right now."

Ron and Gus returned to the building and resumed helping us move the line up the stairs.

We got to the first floor and washed down the floor in front of us. Lt. Mundi told me to shut the nozzle off, so that we could check for gasoline on the second floor.

We all took out our flashlights and checked out the floor, being careful of booby traps, (holes cut out in the floors.) There weren't any signs of gasoline poured on the floor so we proceeded to the upper floors and checked them out, but we found holes cut out on the third and fourth floors. The holes were cut directly underneath each other, we also noticed containers with gasoline placed by the holes cut out in the floors. I guess they knew the fire would extend upwards causing it to ignite the gasoline.

"Can you believe this, I said" I thought firefighters were the heroes, saving lives and property. But we are treated like the enemy." What is this? an extension of Viet Nam?"

The other fires were starting to come under control, so since we were one of the last fire companies on the scene and had a busy district ourselves, the Chief told us to take up and return to quarters. Lt. Mundi radioed Charlie and told him to shut down, we're taking up. We opened up the nozzle and washed down the stairs, with the water that was left in the hose, then grabbed the lengths as we went down the stairs to the street. We each drained a length of hose and folded them up and tied them, and then carried them back to the Pumper.

What a night so far. When we got back into quarters we all headed for the kitchen and put a pot of coffee on and took a deserved break. When we got back to quarters we had a relocated company covering us. It was Engine 212 from Greenpoint. They were anxious to get back to Greenpoint after being at an all hands tonight (3 engines and 2 trucks). and we were anxious to get back into our quarters to take break. Things quieted down for the rest of the tour. Even the enemy needs sleep.

"LIVE BY THE SWORD, DIE BY THE SWORD"

Wintertime on Scholes street is quiet, except for the narcotics trafficking going on in some buildings on the street. Jose' Sanchez, a known drug pusher in the area is seen going in and out of a couple of buildings on the street. The word is out that he has been involved with a lot of crimes connected to his drug pushing.

People have been mugged, shot, stabbed.

Apartments and homes ransacked because of this individual. But nobody will testify against him, for fear of reprisals.

One day while Ron Hinks was on house watch, a car pulls up across the street from quarters and parks in a no parking zone that was lined out so that we could exit and back the Engine into quarters. Ron wasn't aware of this because the apparatus floor doors were closed. But Ron thought he'd take a look out side because he heard a car out front. Sure enough a car was parked there, with no driver. The vehicle would be in the way if we had an alarm and is in the

NO PARKING zone. Ron, yells up to Capt. Sheer, " Hey Cap, can you come down here for a second! "Yeah, what's up Ron? Ron replies," Look out of the front window, we have a car parked out in front of quarters across the street. The driver has to be blind not to see the no parking zone that he or she is parked in."

"Yeah, I see it the Capt. replies. Wait a couple of minutes, maybe the driver will be back . Give him a warning and tell him to move the car.

With this Ron opens the little door and looks around up and down the street.

Looking down the street he sees a man arguing with the neighborhood drug pusher, Jose Sanchez. The man arguing with Jose walks away and starts down the street towards the illegally parked vehicle. Ron says to himself, this must be the person who owns the automobile. Meanwhile the Captain comes down the stairs for a look see.

The man walks to the automobile and starts to open the door. At this, Ron yells over to him. "Hey fellow, can't you see that your in a no parking zone".

The man yells back at Ron with profanities and pulls out a gun and points it at Ron.

Ron seeing the gun dives into the open doorway and yells out to the members.

"He's got a gun, the nut has a gun". With that the Capt. jumps in to the cab of the Engine and calls the Brooklyn dispatcher and tells him to send the cops over to 216's quarters right away, " We have a nut outside threatening us with a gun".

In five seconds you could hear the sirens in the distance, the 90 precinct wasn't too far away. Meanwhile the members heard the auto outside start its engines and then rubber squeaking the vehicle took off. Ron took a peak outside and yelled back to the members. " He's gone, the nut is gone.

In another five seconds New York's finest pulled up with three squad cars, and then a van with a swat team a couple of minutes afterwards.

The Capt. related to the police what happened, and that the man took off in his car when he heard the sirens in the distance. The police Lt. said to the

Capt. laughing. " Pretty soon were going to have to arm you guys, and issue you bullet proof vests to wear under your turnout coats." The Capt. replied "Sounds like a good idea."

A couple of days pass by, and I'm back in on a night shift. Its a about 3:00 in the a.m. Frank Shultz a robust Dutchman is on house watch duty and hears a banging on the front door of the quarters, and a faint cry for help. Frank say's to himself ,Who could this be? Frank opens the door cautiously. As soon as he opens the door a man steps in. " What the hell," Frank yells out, Frank recognizes the man. Its Jose'Sanchez, and he has a knife sticking in his chest.

Jose says " Please help me" and then falls to the floor. Frank yells out, "Engine 216, Turn Out. We all scramble from the bunk room to the apparatus floor to see Frank, kneeling by this man on the floor. Then we all saw the knife protruding from his chest and his shirt soaked with blood. Frank said, It's Jose',the drug pusher from up the street. Lt. Mundi called the Brooklyn dispatcher and said we needed an ambulance and the police over at Engine 216 right away. Jose' didn't make it, he died before the ambulance arrived at quarters. There wasn't any remorse over the loss of Jose', he was a bad guy and caused a lot of suffering to people in the neighborhood.

It is written " If you live by the sword you will die by the sword."

"ST. PATRICKS DAY PARADE"

March, 17, 1969 is a beautiful day, sunny, cool, a perfect day for a parade to honor St. Patrick. I being part Irish, along with other ancestral lineage that I am also proud of. I couldn't wait to get together with some of the members of Eng. 216, and 108 truck to take part in the parade on 5th. Ave., New York City.

We all gathered at a specific location with the rest of our brothers of the FDNY it was around 57th street and 5th Ave. The members of Engine 216 and 108 Truck were grouped together on the sidewalk talking up a storm and having a good time, when I notice a familiar face walking a poodle dog coming our way, I said to myself " damned if it isn't the famous movie producer, Otto Preminger.

Hey guys I yelled out, look, Otto Preminger." Everybody looked up and spotted Otto Preminger walking along with his pooch. Hey Otto, one of the guys yelled out . " How are you doing today? Just fine men,he answered, nice day for a parade. He gave us a wave,and went on his way.

People started to gather by the thousands getting a spot to stand or sit along the along the way.

127

The wearing of the green was prevalent as one looked up Fifth Ave. Along the parade route.

It was almost time to get started as the Emerald Society pipers began to warm up. The sound of the bagpipes sent a thrill up my spine with the drummers hitting their cadence. I thought how this was for centuries back in the old country, when men prepared for battle and the pipes rang out and encouraged them, Duty, Honor, Courage. " OK men", A shout rang out, let's line up and get ready to march. We all got to our positions and got ready to go. We were altogether, firefighters of all ethnic backgrounds. Irish, Italian, Polish, German etc., getting ready to march and to honor the Great St. Patrick, and have a great day. We finally started to march and the fire department Emerald Society pipers started playing. I was proud to be a member of New York's bravest.

The avenue looked green as far as the eyes could see. As we passed the bystanders buy, they would cheer us, and the ladies would throw us kisses.

I thought of all the brothers that we have lost and the brothers who were seriously injured and had to end their careers. I also wondered about myself, being with one of the busiest companies in the city. I quickly put the thoughts out of my mind, and said to myself. " I'm in God's hands."

We were getting to the end of the parade at 86' th Street, we were all looking forward to cold beer, hamburgers and hotdogs at the reception center.

After guzzling down a couple of beers and downing a two or three hotdogs.

The guys wanted to hit a couple of Taverns before we headed home.

The first Tavern we hit was jumping with firefighters, and in the mist of them were a bunch of off duty nurses from a hospital near by. We all got a place at the bar and ordered beers for us all.

A couple of the brothers left the bar and went over to converse with the nurses.

As I was drinking my beer I noticed in a far corner what looked like a big camera on a platform and scanning everybody in the Tavern. I then realized that it was one of the T.V. stations getting ready for the evening news. I then noticed a lady with a mike in her hands going around to individuals and asking questions.

Damn, I said to myself, The brothers are going to get caught live on the 6:00 O'clock news talking to the nurses. Quickly I went over to them and warned them about the cameras, but it was to late they were on Television in living color. I said to myself, I hope the wives aren't watching the TV tonight.

When we all got back to the firehouse to get our cars to go home, the brothers on duty were laughing so hard, their face's were turning blue. We looked at them and almost in unison said, "What in the hell are you guys laughing about?"

Laughing ,one of the brothers said, you guys looked good on TV, especially with the nurses, and your wives were ringing the phone off the hook. You're all in big trouble with the little ladies at home. Ha, ha. You might be better off sleeping here tonight.

We all looked at each other and knew we were in deep trouble with our better halves. And started to think of excuses to give to the wives.

We would never live this down, as the word spread throughout the Battalion.

"JUST A BLAST OF WATER"

Engine 216 turned out to a " All Hands " (One Alarm fire) It was a fully involved four story unoccupied vacant frame dwelling . We wer e third due at the scene of the fire and two Engine Companies andtwo Truck Companies were already at the scene.

The chief in charge ordered us into an six story multiple dwelling that was next to the building on fire. Lt. Mundi ordered us into the building and set up a line. Joe Cass, Frank O'Malley, John Rossi and I set up a line in the fourth floor stairwell. We set up the line by a window over looking the fire. It was a good vantage point.

It was an easy job, all we had to do was direct the stream of water on the building, and knock down the fire. The fire was considered an out side job, which meant that nobody was to operate inside the building, just protect the exposures surrounding the structure on fire.

We got ourselves set and the Lt. ordered the chauffeur Charlie Benni to start water. We opened up the nozzle and the water blew out towards the fire building and hit it broadside.

We couldn't believe our eyes, just as the stream of water hit the building.

Andrew Ashurst

The building started to move away from us, it started to shudder and quake as it moved away from us.

Everybody operating at the opposite side of the building cleared away as the building started to shift.

The structure collapsed and pancaked, and the fire that involved the whole building was gone and the only thing left burning was a pile of rubble in a middle of a lot.

As we poured water on what was left of the building I yelled out to the guys, we did it, we knocked out the fire with a single blast from our line.

Lt. Mundi started laughing, and we all followed suit. It was the funniest thing to happen to us in a while. Nobody was hurt at the fire and the exposed buildings were out of danger.

"A TRAGEDY FOR A LADY IN WHITE"

It was a day shift and it was quite a cool sunny fall day. It's amazing how the fire duty decreases when the kids are in school.

We were in our new quarters with 108 Truck and the 35th Battalion. We were also with the 90 Police Precinct who had their quarters next door .

The apparatus doors were wide open, and a couple of us guys from the Engine and the Truck were hanging out by the door talking.

We all looked to the right when we noticed a pretty nurse with blonde hair walking towards the firehouse.

One of the guys from the truck said " Hey look at this coming our way?

What a doll. The nurse walked up to us and introduced herself to us.

She asked us were the closest subway station was because she needed to take the train into Manhattan.

Almost in unison we said, "O yes, it's on the next corner." But we warned her not to go there, because it was not safe for her, and that we would call a cab for her.

She replied oh it's OK fellas, it's day time and I'm not really worried. I'm sure I'll be OK. She thanked us all, and asked us to take care, and walked towards the subway station . We all watched her as she disappeared down the steps on the next corner. We were all concerned about her safety, but couldn't leave the firehouse and escort her to the subway because at any time an alarm may come in.

We started talking about what a good looking gal she was. I don't think we were talking more than two minutes. When we see the same nurse staggering up the stairs from the subway station holding her eye with her hands and crying for help.

We yelled to the firefighter on housewatch duty and told him we'll be right back, there's an emergency that we have to tend to.

We quickly ran down to the nurse, who was in distress she had her hand covering her eye and we could see that she was bleeding profusely from the area of her eye.

We quickly picked her up and rushed her to the fire house. When we got her to the firehouse we immediately got her into the Chief's call. We called the Chief out and explained to him what had happened and that she needed to get to the hospital right away. The Chief said no problem. His chauffeur jumped into the car.

As we tried to comfort her as she explained that two men hit her in the face and grabbed her purse down in the subway station. At this time the men turned out from the Engine and the Truck to see what was going on.

We called the police next door and explained to them what had happened to the nurse. The Chief called out, OK fellas, I got to get her to the hospital.

The sirens on the Chief's car blared as the vehicle jumped out into Union Ave. on the way to the hospital.

Later on we got the word that the nurse lost the sight of her eye.

Words cannot express the anger that we had for those individuals who mugged that poor nurse. If we had the chance to grab them, I think we would have hung them from the top of the brass pole. That incident bothered us for a long time. It was a sad day for us all.

Andrew Ashurst

A BARBER'S CHAIR FOR THE FIREHOUSE

I was the fire house barber, I had a stool up in the locker room where I cut the brothers hair.

I enjoyed cutting hair for the brothers. It was like our own private barber shop.

And the best thing was that, the haircuts were free. I always wished that I could have a real barbers chair to cut hair with.

One day the truck company got called out to an alarm, the engine company wasn't on this alarm assignment and we remained behind. The truck company had a larger response area then us and many times they went to fires that we didn't go to unless the fire went to a second alarm or better.

It was a nice summer day and I decided to stay out front by the house watch desk and chew the fat with Fr. Gus Landi who was on housewatch duty. The Apparatus floor doors were open and one had a nice view up and down the street.

The 90 police precinct was next door, and always busy. It was always interesting to see some of the characters they would bring in. Across the street from the firehouse was a Kentucky fried chicken

136

place. I'll never forget the time a few months back when we ordered some fried chicken.

We dished out the chicken but there was a piece that had a strange look to it. It didn't have the familiar look as a leg, breast or a wing. Then one of the bothers yelled out " Damn" you know what that is. No, what is it I answered,

Frank O'Malley started laughing, and then got angry,

It's a mouse, its a Kentucky Fried Mouse. And as we looked closer, our stomachs started to turn. Franks right, it's a mouse, its a damned mouse .

Till today, whenever I have fried chicken out, I check every piece to make sure it's chicken.

The truck company was on its way back from the fire, and I could see it coming down Union Ave a couple of blocks away. When 108 truck got to the intersection by the firehouse they gave us a blast with the air horn. A couple of the men were standing on the turntable of the ladder and yelling out to me . " Andy", look what we 've got."

When they pulled up in front of quarters, I couldn't believe my eyes. There standing on the turntable of the ladder was the most beautiful barbers chair that I ever seen.

They backed the rig in, and when the truck stopped I jumped up on the turntable to admire the chair. " Where did you guys get this beautiful chair?" I was like a kid with a new toy. Well this is the story Andy. We had a fire, and it was in a barber shop. Almost everything was destroyed except for this barbers chair. So when we knocked down the fire and finished overhauling the job the owner of the shop came in.

He was of course upset, but said he has insurance and will rebuild the shop with new equipment. We asked him if we can have the chair? And the man said, "It's yours". So we all thanked the barber, grabbed the chair and put it on the Truck.

We took the chair down from the truck and set it up in the recreation room. I said, "This is great guys,"now I can cut hair in style. All we need next is a mirror. One of the brothers from the truck said," One thing at a time Andy, one thing at a time.

Pudgy yelled out , " I need a hair cut." Jump right up Pudge I responded, glad to be of service to you.

"THIS FIRE STOPS HERE"

We were first due at Grand Street and Union Ave. We couldn't believe our eyes. Both sides of Grand Street were on fire, for a whole block. How could there be so much fire all at once?

It was obvious it was arson and accelerants had to be used. The 35th. Battalion called in a 5th alarm .

A lot of companies would be needed right away to stop the fires from spreading rapidly.

Luckily there were no multiple dwellings involved at this point, only ta payers(stores with apartments above) and other commercial stores.

Most of the taxpayers had a common cockloft and the fire spread rapidly from one section to the next. Because the fire was in the daytime all of the occupants of the apartments were out safely.

Engine 216 was assigned to a corner building that was an un-occupied commercial building the fire was trying to spread from the building next door to our position. We took our line up to the top floor and got ready to pour the water on as the truck company pulled the ceilings with their hooks,

When the truckies pulled the ceiling, the fire blew out over us.

The fire was blowing into the rafters and tried to reach down to us, the smoke condition was getting worse by the seconds. We could feel the heat radiating from the walls as the fire next door got worse. We opened up the nozzle and started hitting the fire, the fire seemed to rage when we hit it with the water.

We got word that a building across from us collapsed with a company of men operating in it.

We were operating for about ten minutes, when were heard a yell from downstairs.

"216 how are you doing? Captain Scheer responded , "We're hanging on, who wants to know.

Appearing at the doorway was our Chief of the 35th. Battalion. The Chief said to us all " The fire stops here 216" . Capt. Scheer asked the Chief about the men who were involved in the collapse across the way. The Chief said, they're

OK, they were in the basement and none of the falling debris hit them, thank God. With that the Chief left to check on the other companies in his command.

The Capt. said, "You heard the Chief guys, the fire stops here".

So far the exposures on the other side of the intersection looked good and we don't want this fire spreading over there.

We started to knock down the fire in the ceiling and could hear truckies operating on the roof , cutting holes to vent the roof. We could also hear companies next door to us, they were knocking down the fire and pushing black grey smoke through the rafters.

After we killed the fire, the truckies pulled the ceilings and walls and checked for hot spots. When the hot spots were encountered we washed them down. After checking the area well the Capt. said, " It looks like everything is under control up here". The Capt. radioed Fr. Walsh our pumper operator and told him to shut down the line.

We all pulled together and got the line downstairs and out into the street.

I couldn't believe my eyes when I took a look around. Grand Street was not the same. Some of the stores that I have shopped in were totally gutted.

Especially the old Pawn shop. It was at this old Pawn shop that I purchased my first shotgun to go small game hunting with. It was an old J.C. Higgins 12 gauge shotgun, and I still have it today.

"HELL" LINED UP AGAINST THE WALL

It was a autumn evening 1969 and Engine 216 just returned from a false alarm.

Lt. Mundi tells Charlie Benni to drive over to Mesarole Street because we've got to check out a couple of vacant buildings over there.

Driving down Mesarole St. we can spot the old fires that we had by looking at the burned out frames on the windows, and plywood nailed to close them off.

Vacant tenement building were in the same shape, and ready to be set on fire again by the neighborhood vandals. The area was beginning to look like a science fiction movie, like one of those movies that depicts a town dying, and the buildings are all boarded up and rubbish in the streets.

Lt. Mundi tells Charlie to stop here in front of this taxpayer building.

The store was empty and boarded up. The apartment on the second floor was vacant and had no windows.

The Lt. said, Andy you and John Cass go upstairs and take a look around the premises.

As John and I jumped off the back step of the Engine, Ron Hinks and Tony Amito yelled out to us, " Have fun guys". John and I walked over to the door way. I turned the knob on the door to see if it was open. To my surprise it was open. John and I broke out our flash lights and started up the stairs. It was kind of strange making it up a stairway in a dark vacant apartment with two beams of light in front of us. And the strangest thing was, we weren't pulling any hose.

We got to the landing and walked on to the floor. John and I searched the room we were in and saw nothing but bare walls and floors with news paper thrown about.

Let's check out the rear John maybe we'll find a bag of gold on the floor

"Yeh, sure, just us, right Andy. This would be the last place in the world to find a bag of gold." We walked into a kitchen that was in pretty bad shape, it had old wooden cabinets painted white and probably needed a paint job 5 years ago. The faucet on the sink was dripping lightly and stained the tub with rust. John said ."It doesn't look like anything to be concerned within here let's go up to the front room and check that out." Sounds good I replied.

John moved out of the room ahead of me shining his flash light in front while I followed shining my light on the ceilings and the walls. We entered the front room and walked over to the front windows. We looked down to the engine and spotted Ron , Tony and Lt. Mundi standing by the rig and talking.

I turned my flash light on the wall left of us, and then down to the floor.

What I saw alarmed me, John look at this, John turned and put the beam of his light on what I spotted on the floor. I'll be damned said John Rossi.

Lined up along the wall was twenty five to thirty Molotov Cocktails with wicks and all ready to go. I said to John " I wonder who these were meant for.

John Rossi sticks his head out of the window and yells down to the men.

Hey you guys you'll never believe what we found"?

Lt. Mundi yells back, " What's that John" ?

Come on up a see for yourself guys. Lt. Mundi, Tony Amito and Ron Hinks scurry to the door and scramble up the stairs with there flash lights beaming on the walls as the run up the stairs.

Ok, What's up guys says Lt. Mundi yells out as he gets to the floor. In here, I yelled to the guys. Lt. Mundi walked in along with Dal and Tony. John Rossi said to them .

"Look here on the floor".

"I 'll be a Son of a ———— Lt. Mundi yelled out" Molotov Cocktails. "Yeh,

I said, and they're probably meant for us."

Tony said, " These cocktails probably belong to the gang who have been burning up a lot of buildings in the district.

Lt. Mundi said " I got to call in the Arson Squad on this. Maybe they can get prints off these bottles." Yeah, Ron answers, Maybe they can set up a watch, to see who comes here looking for the cocktails.

Lt. mundi said " The gang probably knows we're in here now. Lt. Mundi said, its a good thing that I decided to check this place out. I had a funny feeling about this place. Now I know why. Can you guys imagine what could have happened with this stuff. Yes, I said. Maybe we saved some lives . Especially our own.

145

NO MORE SPARE PARTS
FOR YOU GUYS

One night Engine 216 and 108 Truck got called out for an auto fire. It was a routine auto fire, about our fifth one for the night. When the companies pulled into this block we spotted the auto right away. It was a brand new Caddy, and smoke was bellowing out of the windows. The fire really didn't really get under way as yet. Usually when we get a call for an auto fire, when we arrive at the scene, the fire is blowing skyward and the auto is completely involved. There was something odd about this fire.

The Engine and the Truck pulled up near the fire and we pulled off the booster hose to get ready to hit the fire. But we noticed something odd at the scene. A few cars up from the Caddy on the opposite side of the street we noticed a bunch of guys sitting in a Caddy just like the one that had been on fire. We paid no mind to it at this time because we had to put the fire out. The truck vented the windows on the auto and fire leaped out of the windows. We opened up the nozzle on the booster hose and moved in on the fire broad side, because attacking a fire to the rear of an auto is dangerous, because of the gas tank. If the tank should blow it would send a fire ball out from the rear of the vehicle and engulf whoever may be at the rear of the vehicle.

After we knocked down the fire the 108 opened the hood of the auto to check for fire.

One of the brothers from 108 came over to us and motioned us to look across the street at the other Caddy, and said" Isn't it strange that Caddy is exactly like this one. It's like those guys setting in that Caddy are waiting for us to get out of here. Two to One they stole that Caddy, set the fire and pulled the alarm to get us over here real quick before the fire really got under way. You know what this is, "Midnight Auto Sales"

Look, this Caddy is totaled already. Why should we leave them parts to take when we leave the scene. Maybe this will discourage the thieves from stealing cars and torching them in our district. We all chimed in, sounds good to us. So Engine and the Truck proceeded in ventilating the auto to let the heat and smoke out and doing a search under the hood for hot spots. Of course the tires had to be ventilated also.

About this time the occupants sitting in the Caddy started to go bananas as we started to ventilate the vehicle.

When we were done with the ventilation of the engineawe hit the auto one more time with water. We then reeled in the booster hose while the officer of the engine reset the alarm box at the corner.

When the Lieutenant returned back to the engine we all took off, back to the firehouse.

But we had company. Following us was the Caddy, the occupants of the Caddy had their heads out of the auto and yelling at us @#!* with language that would melt the Caddy they were in. It looked like trouble, but they soon took off and disappeared into the darkness from which they came.

From then on, fires in ADVs (Abandoned Derelict Vehicle) slowed down a bit.

MY OWN AUTOMOBILE IS STOLEN AND TORCHED

July 24 1969. It was the night that Apollo X1 was going to land on the moon. I was off duty that night. My wife and I like most Americans that night had or eyes glued to the T.V. It was about 11: 30 at night when my wife Chris said to me. " Andy doesn't that sound like our car ?" I listened for second . I remembered that I had a bad muffler on the car, and the car outside sounded like it had a bad muf fler. I jumped off the couch and ran to the door. Just as I opened the door I saw my car pull away from the curb.

I ran outside and watched as another car pulled out just behind it.

I quickly ran next door to my neighbor Jim Nielson and banged on the door . Jin came to the door quickly because he was most likely watching the Apollo X1 landing also. " Jim I cried out, They just stole my car. They pulled away about 30 seconds ago and were headed towards Flatbush Ave.. Jim was a Lieutenant on the Job and worked in a Firehouse just five minutes from here. Jim said hurry jump in my car, and we'll head down that way. Maybe they'll try to go over the Marine Parkway Bridge and that how we'll nail them. If we see them at the toll gate we can stop real quick and alert the police and they'll have a chance to grab them in Rockaway. I don't think they'll take the Belt Parkway because the can be spotted on the Parkway once we alert the police.

When we arrived at the Toll booth we couldn't spot the car. We told the toll booth operator what happened and he got on phone right away and notified the police for us.

I gave the toll booth guy the make and year of the vehicle. It was a 1962 Caddy Coup Deville and the color was black.

I started to think back when I first purchased that auto. A neighbor of mine owned the Caddy. And I asked him if he was ever thinking of selling the car, to see me first.

He said I'm thinking of retiring from the restaurant business soon and I may sell the car and I'll let you know, ok. A few weeks went by and my neighbor knocks on the door.

He said that he decided to sell the car, and if I'm interested it's yours to buy. He gave me a good deal on the Caddy and I purchased it.

My mind jumped back to the present and Jim Nielson said to me, "Andy I don't think there's much that we can do know. It's in the hands of the police. Let's head back home."

While driving back home with Jim, I said " Well the car is a hot potato now, maybe they'll dump the car and take off." Jim said back, " That's possible Andy we'll see."

When we arrived back at home our wives were standing outside with some other neighbors . We pulled up in front of the house, and no sooner did we get out of the car the phone rang inside the house. I answered the phone and it was the police. They told me that they found the car, but the bad news is the thieves set fire to your car. They told me where the car was, and it was only about five minutes from the house in some lot.

Jim and I quickly got in his car and drove to the scene. When we arrived at the scene of the fire. I saw that the car was totally gutted. My heart sunk. Engine 309 was on the scene. They had a booster hose stretched and the fireman holding the nozzle said to me

"Andy is this your car? " I looked at the man who seemed to know me and it turned out to be an old friend of mine from my old neighborhood. I said "John what a surprise, when did you come on

151

Andrew Ashurst

the Job. John replied, a couple of years ago. John said " It's a shame this reunion couldn't be under better circumstances. I told him that Jim and I were also on the Job and that I was with Engine 216 and Jim was a Lieutenant with Engine 321 in the same Battalion as 309. John looked over to Jim and recognized him. "Yes I know Lt. Nielson". I said to John all the flaming Caddy fires that I put out.

I never thought I'd see my Caddy up in flames.

It was the last Caddy that I would ever buy. Especially with no garage to keep it in.

Jim and I drove back home just in time to see Apollo X1 land on the moon.

"A BURST LINE"

An alarm came in for Lee and Hayward St. Engine 216 turned out

.

In 30 seconds we could smell the smoke as we approached the fire. Ladder 108 came in right behind us as we approached the scene of t he fire. Our chauffeur Phil the Greek pulled up to a hydrant about ten yards from the building on fire. We all jumped off the rig and started to stretch the line to the building. The building was a wood frame four story walkup with asphalt shingle, a real matchbox. And was also occupied. The fire was on the fourth floor and blowing out of the windows.

Capt. Scheer was the first to go in. Carmine Santana was on the nozzle, Shawn Sullivan backed up Carmine, Frank O'Malley and I helped stretch the line up the stairs. The forcible entry team of 108 truck went up the stairs first. We got the line up to the fire floor. It was a narrow stairway with a wooden bannister winding up to the top floor.

And it was crowded up on the landing. There was barely any room for the truckies of 108 to step aside as they forced the door open to the apartment on fire.

We got set, Frank O'Malley and were on the landing below handling the line when we were ready to move in on the fire Capt. Scheer kneeling along with Carmine and Shawn yelled to the Greek start water through his handy talky. The water started rushing through the hose and stiffened the hose as it worked its way up to us.

108 yelled out." Are you guys set? Yeh, Lets go. 108 forced the door open and quickly got down to the side. Just as Carmine got ready to open the nozzle there was a blast as the nozzle blew away from the hose. It was a burst line, and every body on the landing on the fire floor bailed out over the bannister to get away from the fire. And they all came down on top of O'Malley and me.

The fire blew out of the apartment out across the landing to the stairway.

The Capt. yelled through the handy talky to the Greek to shut down the line because the line had burst at the nozzle.

We all got the hell out of there real quick, before we roasted.

We got down a floor below and disconnected the burst line as Shawn went out to grab another nozzle. Shawn was back in a jiffy. We placed the new nozzle on the line. We then gathered up enough hose to move in on the fire. Capt Sheer called the Greek to start water again.

The water came blowing through the line as we got ready to move in on the fire again.

The fire was half way down the fourth floor stairs as we moved up hitting it.

After a few minutes we were able to push the fire back towards the apartment.

We knocked down the fire as 108 Truck went in for a search and overhaul.

Luckily we found no victims . The apartment was vacant.

For the first time in my life I realized how a pro football player feels like on the scrimmage line, when they're stacked on top of each other to hold the line.

"A BUILDING COLLAPSES"

An Alarm comes in for South 4thSt and Hewes street Engine 216 turns out.

The fire is about a block away from us and we can smell smoke as we pull out of quarters.

The building is a vacant six story tenement building.

Eng. 216 pulls up to a hydrant near the building as 108 Truck pulls in front of the building and drops its out riggers to stabilize the truck. Then raises it's ladder to the roof of the building

There isn't any fire showing in front of the building and it looks like it's all in the rear of the building The 35th. Battalion pulls up alongside 108 Truck. The Chief gets a quick assessment of the fire as the Capt. Of 108 Truck tells the Chief that the whole rear of the structure is on fire and the exposures surrounding the structure are in jeopardy.

The Chief quickly sends in a 3rd. Alarm assignment to get more companies on the scene.

Lt. Mundi tells us to stretch a line up to the third floor.

Frank O'Malley, Gus Landi, Ron Hinks, Tony Amito and I grabbed loops of hose off the back of the engine and start stretching into the hallway and then up the stairs.

Engine's 237,221 and Engine 206 are now arriving as we stretch our line into the building. Engine 206 is assigned to stretch it's line into the second floor to knock down the fire in the rear. Engine 221 stretches up behind us to the third floor and starts attacking the fire in the apartments on the left side in the rear of the building. Ladder 104 enters the building and starts operating. The whole 35th Battalion is now operating in this building.

Every floor of the building was on fire in the rear. And had men operating on them. The members of Engine 216 were all on our knees moving forward and pushing the fire back towards the vented windows. The plaster on the ceiling above was breaking and falling on us.

The heat and the smoke was tremendous as moved in on the fire. Shortly after operating on the roof, The members of 108 Truck were ordered off the roof because it was in the danger of collapse. 104 Truck is searching the floors for victims and possible derelicts that may have been in the building.

Andrew Ashurst

The Chief of the 35th. Battalion comes to the third floor to see how we are progressing with the fire. He yells out and tells us a few words of encouragement and then moves on to check the other floors.

We were starting to get a handle on the fire as the fire was venting most of the heat and smoke out of the rear windows. When suddenly we heard a loud roar and crashing sound.

The fire on the third floor disappeared as we were moving in on it. Ten feet from us the whole rear of the building collapsed, and took the fire down with it.

We all looked up and saw a dark starry night. It was a weird feeling standing and looking out on a floor that seconds ago was totally engulfed with fire.

And suddenly no fire. We shut down the line and the Capt. ordered us to get out of the building before the rest of it comes down. The very next thought that we all had, were the men in the other companies. Did anybody get killed or was anyone seriously injured. When we finally got out of the building. The whole third alarm assignment was out side.

It was a miracle. Not one man was seriously injured, just a few scrapes. When the building collapsed it took the whole rear of the buil

158

ding, pancaking each floor as it collapsed, all the debris stopped on the second floor.

If the floors would have collapsed down any further, the men of Engine 206 would have been under the rubble.

For some reason, the good Lord protected us all that night. We washed down the pile of rubble and put out what was left of the fire.

I guess we were all thinking the same thing, we all may have been buried under it.

AMBUSH AT THE CROSS ROADS

Its summer 1970 and a hot July night and Engine 216 and 108 Truck are running like crazy as usual. Last year Engine 216 was the 23 busiest engine Co.

In response's In New York City, we turned out to 4617 runs that year and had 2281 working fires. We were the 19 busiest Engine Company in working fires In New York City .

Ladder 108 had 5443 runs and 3600 workers. Ladder 108 was the 15th busiest truck company in runs in New York City and the 7th busiest in working fires.

In those day's there were approximately 146 Ladder Companies and 220 Engine Companies in the City of New York.

I wonder if we would out do last years record.

An alarm comes in for South 3rd and Havemeyer Streets. There is fire down the middle of South 3rd. Street all the way to the next intersection. It looks like the people threw the garbage in the middle of the street and set it all on fire.

I looked down the street as we were getting ready to pull in to hook up to a hydrant. But something wasn't right. Something was different, I couldn't make it out at first.

Then it hit me like a wet rag in the face. I yelled to the Lt. Mundi from the jump seat in back of him. "Lou, don't go in.

"Why he yelled back at me". I responded. " Do you remember what happened in Brownsville when an Engine and Truck company pulled in to a situation like this?"

And when they pulled into street the neighborhood gang pushed cars into the ends of each corner and blocked them in.

And when they had them corralled, They threw Molotov Cocktails of the roofs on them and then bricks and cans full of rocks on them. Yeah, Lt. Mundi responded. Well Lou, that's what they're getting ready to do here. Look down the street I yelled back to Lt. Mundi. "Where are all the women and children? And where are the all the teenagers and young men? Lt. Mundi answers me.

"You're right Andy, I don't see them in the streets. I yelled back, "You know where they are, they're on the roofs waiting for us to come in."

161

Lt. Mundi yells over to Charlie Benni our driver. " Don't go in Charlie stay here in the intersection while I contact Engine 221 before they come in on the other side.

Engine 221 was just getting to the intersection on the other side when they got the call from Lt. Mundi warning them of a possible ambush. Engine 221 starts backing out real fast into the intersection. When suddenly, we can see the missiles coming off the roofs like burning rockets coming down out of space towards us. Some of the guys were off the rig and jumped under cover as the Molotov Cocktails exploded around us.

Lt. Mundi yelled out to the men to get back on the Engine, cause we're getting out of here.

Charlie drove the Engine down the street about 100 ft., while Lt. Mundi called in NewYorks Finest. The 90 Precinct wasn't to far away and we should have the troops here any minute.

Sure enough the police started rolling in with sirens screaming. They starting coming out of their squad cars with riot gear and shotguns.

The missiles stopped as soon as they arrived, and the young revolutionaries took off to their hiding places, like rats scurrying to their holes.

When the police got the area under control we resumed our fire fighting duties.

It was starting to get dark and the garbage in the street was lighting up the sky.

Engine 221 came in on the opposite side along with 104 truck. 108 truck was with us on our side.

New York's Finest went up to the roofs of the buildings on each side of the street to make sure the wise guys were gone.

It was a strange feeling putting out that fire in the street, we kind of had a feeling that we were targets down in the street. But we knew our brothers in blue were looking out for New York's Bravest.

My thoughts went back a few months when a covering Lieutenant pulled up to quarters, got out of his car and called us out to look at his car. Apparently somebody shot at him as he was driving his car to quarters, and put a bullet through the hood of his car, and into the firewall inside, missing his body by a couple of inches. It was like we were fighting a guerilla war along with fighting fires.

163

Andrew Ashurst

The Lieutenant was visibly shaken, but settled down after a cup of coffee. One of the brothers said out loud , " I hear there's going to be a sale on armored cars" or maybe we can rent them to come to work in." Everybody broke out laughing at the statement including the young covering Lieutenant.

"FIREHOUSE ROCK"

I can't recall the exact time and the year of the following. But I'll never forget that day.

We were all sitting in the kitchen having coffee and gabbing to each other.

Charlie Benni was lifting weights. Our kitchen was a combo of a rec. room and a kitchen. So far it was a quite day. The alarms coming in were few, but none for us, at the moment.

I was getting ready to take another sip of my coffee when suddenly we heard a blast and the whole fire house shook. I spilled half my coffee on the floor of the kitchen.

"What the hell was that, we all yelled, out almost in unison? "

Capt. Sheer ran down the stairs. And yelled out to us to get our gear on, and stand by for an alarm to come in. We opened the doors to the Fire House, and Charlie, who was our chauffeurs for the day jumped up into the cab of the Engine, and the Captain jumped up along side him in his seat.

We anticipated all the circuits to open, and the alarms to start rolling in, we waited for the call to Engine 216(at that time we were still a single company).

It is already five minutes since we heard the blast that shook our fire house, and nothing came. We didn't even hear an alarm come in for the Division.

We all stood around astonished that no alarms could be heard coming in at all.

One of the brothers even ran down to the corner to see if anything was going on. Looking to the sky for that tell tale sign of black smoke and flames shooting into the sky .No alarms came in., We're all thinking out loud, this can't be. Something big has had to happen in the District, if not the immediate neighborhood. Something big is going on, and we all had the feeling that most likely a plant, or commercial building had an explosion and a lot of people maybe injured, if not killed. And there would be definitely, a lot of fire. And that we would be in the middle of it shortly, and it wasn't going to be good.

The Captain called the Brooklyn Dispatcher and told him about the blast. The dispatcher said calls were coming in all over, from companies about the blast.

The Captain said apparently the blast has raddled quite a few companies, but nothing in their districts.

The Captain told us to stand down. If anything comes up we'll be dispatched. Shortly the dispatcher got back to us. It was bad alright. But the blast originated in Linden New Jersey, and the sound waves traveled across New York Harbor to Brooklyn and Manhattan.

Apparently there was an explosion at one of the oil refineries at Linden, New Jersey.

People were killed a the refinery and the fire was contained to that area.

It was a relief knowing that this one wasn't for us. It made me think about what would happen in case of a catastrophic event, for example a nuclear explosion. The first sound would be a large blast, like today, and then eternity.

Are we ready, are we ready to meet God. I have thought about this seriously lately. Especially when I'm crawling on my hands and feet with an inferno in front of me.

The only thing between me and that inferno is a nozzle, a high volume of water and my Guardian Angel.

There is an old quote that is familiar with a lot of people. It was from an army Chaplin in World War 11. " There are no atheists in fox holes." How true, but what I believe the good Chaplin was trying to say was. Be in God's grace all the time, so that even if you step off a curb and get killed by an automobile, you'll be prepared to face Almighty God.

The Good Merciful Lord only knows how many times I fell out of grace. And he has been patient with me when a fall down a couple of rungs and he lifts me up again.

BOMBERO, BOMBERO, FUEGO, FUEGO
(FIREMAN, FIREMAN, FIRE, FIRE)

It was a week after Thanksgiving 1968, I was a fourth grade firefighter and went hunting up-state New York with a couple of old neighborhood friends of mine. The next morning we got up early, about 5:00 am. We then got to our designated spots in the woods, and settled in.

The sun was just coming up when I noticed movement in front of me about 70 yds. out. I could barely make it out because it was still a little dark. The flash of the bucks tail gave it away. I raised my rifle and checked the area for other hunters. I had a scope on the rifle and put my cross hairs on the buck. He was a beauty, and looked like he had about eight points on his rack. I slowly squeezed the trigger and then click, nothing happened. Squeezed it again, click. What the- - - -.

The Buck looked my way, wagged his white tail and away he went.

I couldn't believe it. My first chance in years to nail a buck and my firing pin breaks.

Andrew Ashurst

I waited awhile then walked back to the cabin and waited for my friends.

It was about 8am and they all started to make their way back to the cabin.

I told the guys what had happened, and they shook their heads. My friend Hank said, that must be the buck I spotted running out away from me about 5:45 this morning.

Its too bad Andy,

I said to the guy's, "I guess that's it for me, my rifle is out of action and I won't be able to hunt. Jack, one of my hunting buddies said back, "Andy, you can come back to the City with me, I have to work tonight" (Jack was a Correction Officer) Great, I said.

So late that afternoon Jack and I left Hank and our other friend Mike. And we headed back to the City. Little did I know that I was in a heap of trouble back home. For when I got back home my wife ran out of the house frantic. "Andy" she yelled to me, I've been trying to get in touch with you, the Battalion Chief was just here and said that you are

AWOL from your firehouse " What, I answered, I'm not supposed to work tonight. I'm working tomorrow night. I looked at my watch
170

and it was 7:15 pm Chris nervously said you had better call your firehouse and let them know you're on your way in. I ran into the house and double checked my work schedule. They were right. I thought I was on a Chinese 72(Every third week we got 72 hours off after our day shift). I really seriously screwed up. I called up quarters and told them what happened. They told me to get in as soon as possible, and that they would call up

The Battalion Chief of 35th Battalion, and tell him that I'm OK.

I kissed the wife and jumped into my car hunting gear and all, and headed for Engine 216. About a half hour ride from the house.

While driving in, I thought of the charges that would be filed against me.

How stupid of me, how could I have screwed up like this. Once the officer on duty listed me AWOL, I was cooked.

When I arrived at quarters I parked the car and jumped into quarters, and entered my name and time of arrival in the log book at the house watch desk..

I explained to the officer in charge what had happened. Thank God, I said to myself.

If that firing pin hadn't broken I would have still been hunting, and Chris wouldn't have been able to get in touch with me. (Cell phones didn't exist then)

Soon enough I received notice to report to Fire Headquarters, downtown Brooklyn.

I was really shaken. I figured my career in the FDNY was over. I was to report downtown Jan.20, at 9:00 am. In dress uniform.

When arrived at the office I knocked on the door and walked in. The secretary asked me to sit down, and told me I should be called in shortly to see the Chief.

In five minutes the Chief came to the door and said, "Fireman Ashurst, you can come in now". I got up and walked in saluted the Chief. You can stand at ease Ashurst, while I look at this documentation. The Chief looked up to me and said, Can you please explain what happened? I explained to the Chief what happened that morning in question, and that I had honestly got mixed up with my schedule, and that it wouldn't happen again. The Chief looked at me and said, " You, have to be more careful Ashurst, try not to let this happen again". I'm going to have to dock you a day off your vacation.

Yes, Sir I replied, (the weight of the world just rolled off my shoulder).

OK Ashurst the Chief said, you can go now. And be careful, you're with a very busy fire company. Yes Sir, I replied, I saluted the Chief and walked out of the office.

And with a sigh of relief, I headed for the first phone available and called the wife to let her know the results of the meeting and that everything turned out okay.

Feeling like a new man I headed back to Williamsburg, Brooklyn to the firehouse.

It was about 11:00 in the morning and I was approaching the corner of Scholes St.

And Union Ave. The fire house was just around the corner.

Suddenly an Hispanic man runs across the intersection towards me yelling, Bombero,

Bombero, Fueago, Fueago. Fireman, Fireman, Fire, Fire . I yelled back to the man who was besides himself. Where, where is the fire? In the building down the street,he cried back to me.

I told him to run down to the building and wait in front of it while I go and get help right away. The first thing was to get to the alarm box on the corner. This would turn out the companies right away. I ran to the corner and pulled the lever on the Alarm box. Next I ran down to the building as fast as possible.

When I got to the building I saw it was a six story tenement, I didn't notice any smoke showing in the front at all. The civilian yelled out to me, " Inside, Inside.

I ran into the hall way and sure enough the fire was blowing out of an apartment by the stairwell with the fire blowing up the stairs and trapping the people on the upper floors. I said to myself, no one is going to be able to get out of their apartments.

I then quickly ran out of the building to the front. I spotted the fire escape ladder It had to be at least 9 feet in the air, hooked in position on to the fire escape. I said to myself, I've got to get up to that ladder and drop it.

As I was getting ready to make a leap for the ladder one of the residents yelled to me and told me that there was a woman and a baby living on the first floor.

I backed up and made a running leap for the ladder and made it to first rung.

I pulled myself up the ladder to the first floor. I yelled down, " Watch out,

I unhooked the ladder and dropped it down to the ground below, then headed for the window.

I pulled up on the window, and it opened, thank God. The smoke came billowing out as I climbed in, crawling on the floor. "Hello, Hello, I yelled out, is anybody here?

Suddenly I hear screaming in another room. With a voice choking," My baby, my baby" please help me. Keeping low, I crawled to the room where the voice came from and found a young woman trying to get her baby out of a crib.

Don't worry, don't worry, I'll help you. When she noticed me in my uniform she cried out thank God, bombero thank God.

I grabbed the baby and put the baby in one arm and grabbed the arm of the woman and told her to get low to the floor as we made it to the window. I got the mother out of the window and handed the baby to her.

By that time people were gathering down at the ground. I then yelled to a man , to come up the ladder and take the baby, and help the mother down the fire escape.

175

I then shot up the fire escape to the third floor.

The third floor window was opened with smoke pouring out. I could hear the fire companies turning out. They were on the way.

I climbed into the window and got down low on the floor and started to yell for anybody that may be in the apartment.

Sure enough two women come crawling on the floor towards me.

"Our dog , our dog is in here, please find him. I yelled back to them. " Forget about the dog, your lives are in danger, I have to get you out off this building right away.

Thinking to myself, if the fire blows out of the floor below, we could be trapped on the fire escape, because fire escapes on the front of the buildings don't go to the roof.

We would be roasted alive.

The women yelled out," We won't leave until we find our dog." " OK I yelled back, get to the fire escape I'll look for the dog." The women were big women, I sure as hell would be in trouble getting them out, if they passed out on me.

The two ladies made their way to the fires escape but stood by the window as I searched for the dog. I worked real quick crawling around on my hands a knees looking for the dog. I crawled into what

"CRY FIRE"

looked like a bedroom the smoke was starting to bank down in the apartment, and I didn't know how long I would last. I was getting ready to get out of the room when I spotted a bed. When I stretched my arm under the bed and I I felt the dog. I felt for his collar and pulled him out. He didn't resist I believe the smoke was starting to get to him.

I got him to the window, he was a big white hound dog, and the two ladies were over joyed. Ok ladies we have to get off of this fire escape.

As I helped them down, 108 truck was placing its ladder at the building, Engine 216 already had its line stretched in to the hallway.

I got down to the ground, assisted by the brothers of companies at the scene.

I then ran back to the firehouse, donned my gear, and ran back to 216 and joined them fighting the fire in the ground floor apartment. The Captain was on duty, and was glad to see me on the line with them.

When we knocked down the fire, the members of Engine 216 took up the hose line and returned to the firehouse.

177

The Captain called me upstairs to the office. I was thinking to myself I guess he wants to talk to me about going downtown this morning, to answer the charges against me.

I went up the stairs and knocked on the Captains door. "Come in Andy", the Capt. said, take a load off and have a seat. I grabbed a seat by his desk and anticipated the Captain getting ready to address me.

"Andy, he said. You have had quite a day. First you're downtown because of charges against you, and right after that you're involved with an off duty rescue."

"What happened while you were downtown." Well, I said to the Captain, I was reprimanded and had a day taken off my vacation. And thank God that's all that happened to me." I'm sorry Captain I'll try not to have this happen again." The Captain responds, don't worry about it, we all screw up now and then, we're all not perfect.

Just be careful, ok?" " And by the way Andy, you did a great job this morning at the fire we had. And I understand that you rescued some people out of that building. A woman and a baby and two elderly women and a dog." Yes Captain, I replied. The Captain continued, "You did this without your turnout clothing, and above the fire. You took some chance, especially working off the fire escape

178

above the fire. And then you got back to the fire house and grabbed your turn out clothing, ran back, and joined the company in fighting the fire. The Captain continue " Andy, I'm putting you in for a a rescue, you deserve it. "But Captain I said, I just had charges against me this morning"!

"Don't worry about it, the Captain responded, one thing hasn't got to do with another." " Thank you Captain I responded." The Captain shook my hands and I left the room. I then changed back it my civies. My dress uniform was dirty and had white dog hairs all over it.

When I returned home, my wife Chris noticed my dress uniform all dirty and covered with dog hairs. What happened she said to me. I said to her, you'll never believe it.

MEDAL DAY

June, 1970

This day would be one of the proudest days of my life. It was a beautiful June day, sunny and mild. My wife, her mom and dad and my two children were present along with my Mom and an Aunt of mine. Also present was my old Capt. Who was now a Battalion Chief. Chief Shumacher.

The dignitaries present were. Mayor Lindsey, Fire Commissioner Lowery, Chief of the Dept. O'Hagan and those Officers and Clergy involved with the Medal day Presentation.

All the Medal recipients reported over to an area were we lined up in a column and got ourselves ready to march over to the City Hall reception. The Emerald Society Pipers were in place. Then the drums rang out and the Pipes began to play, sending a chill down my spine. I thought of all the men before me and the men present who have put themselves in danger to help save a life, and those that have sacrificed their lives in the past and the present. I also thought of the widows and the children left behind of those of the past and those now sitting and waiting today at the front steps of City Hall. All the men alongside me today, could have given the supreme sacrifice but for the grace of God were spared. It made me think of my own life, am I prepared to make the supreme sacrifice. This day would change my life forever.

The pipers rang out, and we began to march over to the reception waiting for us at City Hall. When we got close to the reception I spotted my family, and looking intently for our arrival. My son Andy and my daughter Dee spotted me and were waiving and trying to get my attention. I looked their way and gave them a smile.

As soon as we were in place the pipers stopped playing and we were given a round of applause.

Invocation was given by one of the clergy and then the National Anthem was played.

After the National Anthem Fire Commissioner Lowery gave an address. And shortly after, the Mayor gave his address.

The saddest part of the ceremony was the presentation of the Posthumous Medals.

There were seven men who have made that supreme sacrifice and died in the performance of their duties last year. And the medals were given to the their next of kin.

Andrew Ashurst

After this presentation Our Chief of the Dept. John O'Hagan gave an address.

This was followed by a selection given by the Emerald Society Bagpipe Band.

Benediction was given by Msgr. Jablonski who was one of the F.D.N.Y. Chaplins.

Then finally the Presentation of the Remaining Medals and rewards.

In turn I was called up to receive the Mayor LaGuardia Medal. This medal was established in 1937. Mayor Fiorella H. LaGuardia while mayor, was the City of New York's #1 fire fan. He greatly supported the firefighters. It was an honor to receive this medal. But this medal had a special meaning for me. When my mother and my brother and I came to New York from California back in 1941 we were in a desperate situation. A friend interceded for us and the Mayor personally got us aid. It was as if the late Mayor gave me this medal himself.

THE PRIDE OF WILLIAMSBURG

108 TRUCK

What can I say about 108 Truck, our comrades in arms. One of the busiest and best Truck companies in the City of New York. In the hay day of the King Assassination this Fire Company responded to and average of 6000 alarms and 4000 working fires a year.

Have and had in those days some of the best firefighters that the City could produce.

Before moving to their new quarters with us, they had a unique firehouse on Siegal St. Willamsburg Brooklyn.

The firehouse was about eight blocks away from Engine 216 quarters on Scholes Street. 108 had a high ceiling in their recreation room. The ceiling was adorned with various collections of art. Trophies of their hard work and dedication were placed in various places, as objects of art to be gazed upon with pride.

One of the objects of artistic admiration was a parachute that flowed gracefully from the ceiling to the floor, another art piece was a motorcycle hanging from another area of the ceiling. Adorning the

183

floor area was and old fire alarm box, pillar and all, painted fire engine red.

Some of the men were well known throughout the Dept. One such firefighter was Pudgy Walsh.

Pudgy was the coach for the New York City Firefighters Football team. He also managed a team of his own named the Brooklyn Mariners. Pudgy was one of the first guys I meet on my first response to an alarm with Engine 216 and 108 Truck. Pudgy would be one of the last guys I would meet before my career ended with the FDNY. Pudgy would be the one to search for me when I got seriously injured at a fire.

Siegal Street in Wiiliamsburg was a poverty stricken area in Brooklyn of mostly Hispanic population. Drug pushers were present in the area. The men had to keep their vehicles in a gated area so as to protect them damage and thieves.

I'll never forget the day when one of the members of 108 Truck was finishing up a night shift and went to get his car. When this particular firefighter got to his automobile, he found that somebody threw a dog off the roof of the tenement building next door and on to the roof of his automobile, killing the dog, and wrecking his car.

All I know is, all hell broke out on Siegal Street that day.

When 108 Truck made their move to the new quarters with Engine 216, the company wasn't gone a day, when somebody or somebodies set fire to their old quarters.

They say Fort Apache is in the South Bronx. If so, Williamsburg Brooklyn in those day's, had a strong second place.

Some of the area residents were not aware of the well trained firefighters they had at their disposal if they had a fire in their dwellings. That these men would put their lives on the line to protect them. It was a shame to treat us as if we were the enemy.

I have been to many, many fires. And have very rarely had so much as a cup of hot coffee offered to us on frigid days when we were out on the street taking up our lines with the snow and sleet, raddling our bones.

Andrew Ashurst

A FATAL ACCIDENT THAT SHOULD NOT HAVE HAPPENED

It was a hot summer day, and everybody in Williamsburg was out on the fire escape or on the front stoops trying to beat the heat, unless they had air conditioning. And many didn't.

Engine 216 and 108 Truck were as busy as usual putting out automobile fires , garbage fires and an occasional structural fire and numerous false alarms. Going through the streets and looking up to the windows you could spot tots, at the window ledges with fathers or mothers holding them, as far as six stories up. I said to my self " One of these day's we're going to get a call, and find one of those tots on the sidewalk"

Well it happened we got a call to South 3rd and Hooper Street, a child had fallen out of a 6th floor window.

The truck and engine pulled up to the alarm box, people were at the box, and directed us to a rear court yard. When we arrived at the scene of the accident we spotted a young lad no older than 3 years old on the courtyard floor with it's mother holding him and screaming with sorrow.

186

The situation looked bad. The little boy was bleeding from a wound on his head, and from his ears and mouth. The mother of the child let us work on the child, but we knew that the child was already dead, his pupils were completely dilated and there was no response, no pulse and no breathing. We had to work on the child so that the people would know that we cared, until the ambulance came . We decided to put a resuscitator on the child and give him oxygen and make his ground soft with a blanket.

The next thing that happened was, somebody started throwing bottles off the roof on us. This was an outrage. Here we are attending to a little boy, and some devil on the roof is throwing bottles of at us.

One of the men from 108 truck yelled up to the roof and said, " If you don't stop the crap, were leaving this area. At that, a few Hispanic men on the rear firescape yelled up to the people on the roof and raced up the fire escape to the roof after the individuals who threw the bottles at us.

The ambulance arrived, and the ambulance Paramedics took over.

A little boy died, that didn't have to die, if only the parents were not neglectful. This time It was a high price to pay.

Andrew Ashurst

MY CAREER WITH THE FDNY COMES TO AN END

Brooklyn Hospital released me after about a week. Their tests and X Rays were negative. This was a relief for me, for I had no intentions of leaving the job. I was studying for the Lieutenants Exam. Along with one of my best friends, Frank Ryan. Who later on would become a Battalion Chief, and would be involved in the rescue efforts to find victims and our fallen brothers at the at the World Trade Center disaster.

I was assigned to light duty for a few weeks then returned to full duty. I still had pain where I had the injury and didn't think much of it, until we had a fire in a multiple dwelling. The fire was on the top floor (6th floor) During the extinguishment of the the fire the pain in my lower back got intense. I knew that something wasn't right.

When we got back to quarters I told the officer in charge about my back problems.

The next morning I reported to the medical office.

The doctor at the medical office wasn't too convinced that I had a problem, because the hospital reports were inconclusive. He then sent me in to get my back X-rayed. When I entered the room where X- the ray's were being done the Technician told me to lie down on the table and pull my legs into my chest. This would give him a good shot of the spine. I did everything that the Tech suggested. The Tech took a couple of pictures and sent me back to the doctor.

The doctor told me to have a seat until the X-rays came back.

I don't think I was sitting down more than 10 minutes when the Technician enters the doctors office, and addresses the doctor. " Doc, this man has a fracture"

The Doctor responds, " Where?" On his spine, responded the Tech.

The Doctor looks at the X-Rays and with his expression of concern turns to me and say's," I'm sorry Ashurst," I didn't realize. How in the hell did the hospital release you with a spinal fracture is beyond me. I'm sorry but I'll have to place you on limited service." I asked the Doctor, " What is worse, is that I was responding to alarms with that fracture. The doctor shook his head and said, " You're a lucky man, you could have exacerbated the situation.

When I got home from the medical office, my wife knew something was wrong, Chris seen the down look on my face. " What's wrong hun? "She said, I looked at her and said,

"They found a fracture on my spine. One of the Transverse process's on my spine was totally fractured. The Doctor put me on limited duty. That means no more fire duty.

He wants me to keep off my feet as much as possible.

The next day I went to the firehouse to give the report to the Captain. The Captain said he was sorry that this had to happen.

That morning the unthinkable happened. The New York City Firefighters went on strike. First time in the history of the Dept. The strike didn't go more than a day. Mayor Lindsey ordered that three men from every firehouse was to be transferred out . I was one of them. Since I was on limited service it made sense.

This is when I decided to retire. If I couldn't respond to fires anymore I didn't want to be on the job. It wasn't the same. I was still young enough to pursue another career.

The Post Korean War GI Bill was extended for another two years. I decided to take advantage of the extension and go back to school.

I'll never forget the look on my young sons face, and the tears rolling out of his eyes, when I told him I wasn't going to be a firefighter any more. I told him like Gen. Mc Arthur said in his last speech at West Point. Andy my son, Ole Firefighters never die they just fade away. And that is the way it is till this day. I'm an old firefighter who remembers the old day's with one of the busiest firehouses in New York City and the men that I fought fires with. Some have died on the job and some off the job. And some are like me, just fading away.

THE END

About the Author

Andrew Ashurst became a New York City Firefighter in the 1967. After Probationary School he was sent to Engine Company 216 located in the Williamsburg section of Brooklyn, New York.

During the Sixties and Seventies, which were considered the War Years neighborhoods like Williamsburg, South Bronx, Bedford Stuyvesant and the Brownsville areas of New York had a dramatic increase in structural fires, mostly because of arson. There was an increase in riots and crime throughout the City because of racial unrest and turmoil.

Engine 216 became one of the busiest fire companies in the City. In 1970 they responded to 4960 alarms and 2689 working fires for that year.

This book is dedicated to firefighters everywhere, be it professional or volunteer, and to those men with Engine

216, 108 Trucks, 35th Battalion and the 11th Division that I had the honor to work with and to all my brothers of the New City Fire Department who lost their lives in the performance of their duties especially to the Brothers who lost their lives at the World Trades Center September 11, 2001.

This book is also dedicated to all the families of firefighters and emergency response teams everywhere, and especially to those who lost their loved ones in the performance of their duties.

A portion of the proceeds from the sale of this book will be contributed to The New York City Firefighters Burn Unit

These stories are true accounts.

Some of the names of the fire fighters and response areas have been changed.

Printed in the United States
53106LVS00006B/4